A Muzzled Murder

An Amelia Hartford Cozy Mystery

Angie Street

BA Reads

First edition April 2026

Contents

1

A New Day at the Maple Leaf Inn

The bell above the Maplewood Diner door jingles as Edna Hampton steps inside, bringing with her the chill of a late-autumn Kansas morning and the exhaustion of ten hours on the road from Colorado. The smell of frying bacon and strong coffee wraps around her like a long-lost comfort.

Dottie Callahan, queen of the diner and Maplewood gossip, spots her at once. Dottie always does. Her silver hair swept up into a neat bun and lipstick bright enough to be seen from Main Street. She carries herself with the energy of someone who has no intention of slowing down, ever.

"Well, honey, you look like you've wrestled a highway and won," Dottie says, waving her toward a corner booth. "Sit down before the coffee gets cold. I'm Dottie, you need a plate of something hearty? No charge for conversation."

Edna offers a faint, polite smile and slides into the booth. Her travel-creased coat smells faintly of the lavender sachet she packed beside her late husband's Bible. Her hands tremble a bit, though she isn't sure if it is nerves, fatigue, cold, or the memories she carries.

Dottie fills a mug and sets it in front of her. "Passing through, sweetheart, or visiting family?"

Edna hesitates, her eyes fixate on the dark surface of her coffee. "No family here. My son... died here, ten years ago. Hoping to find out why."

The words land heavy, cutting through the easy chatter of the diner. Even the bell above the door seems to fall silent for a beat.

"Oh my, are you Eric's mama?"

Edna nods, her eyes open wide as she looks at Dottie. "How did you know?" she asks.

Dottie places her free hand on Edna's shoulder. "That sort of thing is big news around here. He was a polite young man and it was a tragedy, not something you forget."

"They said it was a hunting accident. I believed it initially. But... after my husband passed, I found some of Eric's things boxed up in the garage. I have been questioning the story ever since," Edna admits. "I just want to understand it, actually, I need to."

Dottie lets out a slow long breath and gently rubs her shoulder. "Oh, honey. You came a long way for some hard truths. But you came to the right place."

"Did you know him well?" Edna asks.

"Just from his visits here, lots of little chats while serving him," Dottie says. "I know Hank Ross well, the previous sheriff. He and Eric were sometimes here together; seemed like Hank was fond of the lad. Honestly, I thought your son's death was sudden and closed up too quick. Hank wouldn't talk about him at all after it happened."

A tear seeps out the corner of Edna's eye. "I thought if I saw where it happened, get more details, I could finally rest."

Dottie tilts her head and sighs, "Sometimes peace comes after you get answers, not before. I can relate," as she rests her hand on Edna's shoulder. "I know someone who you need to visit. Just outside town, at the Maple Leaf Inn. Ask for Amelia Hartford. She's not an official or anything, but she has a knack for digging up the truth."

"An innkeeper?"

"Yes, like I said, not an official, but she has great instincts, she helped the sheriff solve a murder a couple weeks back, one that had the whole town buzzing," Dottie explains, smiling proudly.

Edna wraps her hands around the mug, increasing her grip. "I don't want to cause trouble or drag people into my misfortune."

"Oh, sugar, trouble's already caused," as Dottie tops off her coffee. "You're trying to set it right. Go see her. You won't regret it. She is becoming one of our town jewels," Dottie says as she writes the directions to the Inn on the back of an order slip. "And, she's got herself a dog who's part detective, part local celebrity, plus the sweetest guy ever. His name is Bailey. If nothing else, he'll cheer you up a bit."

Edna stares at the note, looks up at Dottie, "I guess it is worth a try. I just hope I'm not a bother. I do love dogs, but had to leave mine at home."

"Don't worry yourself, you just go see her and tell her Dottie sent you. She'll listen, and my guess is she'll help you find those answers." Dottie starts to leave the table and then turns back, "Hon, did you decide on breakfast or just the coffee?"

"I'll just finish my coffee, not really hungry," as she stares out the window.

Outside the diner, the wind is scattering colorful maple leaves across Main Street. She watches them as they dance and twirl in the breeze. Edna takes one last sip of her coffee and draws a steadying breath. "All right," she murmurs. "I'll go. You said, Amelia, right?"

"Good girl, yes, and you just head out that way," Dottie points to the right. "You can't miss it—a lovely place with a big wraparound porch." Dottie leans close with a conspiratorial wink. "And don't be fooled if Amelia tells you she's retired from sleuthing. Around here, retirement is just what we call a coffee break."

Edna grins ever so slightly and reaches for Dottie's arm, giving it a gentle squeeze, "Thank you. I think I am ready."

The scent of cinnamon and browned butter drifts through the kitchen of the Maple Leaf Inn. Morning sunlight shines through lace curtains, glints off the polished oak counters that her grandmother refinished decades before, when she bought the bed and breakfast and moved to Maplewood, making it her home. Amelia is pleasantly going about her preparation of breakfast for her guests, just as her grandmother did. Mornings are Amelia's peaceful time, baking scones, frying up bacon and eggs, and setting the table before the guests saunter in. The smells calm her, the work focuses her and the memories fill her heart, not only today but every day.

"Bailey, don't you dare."

Her warning almost too late. A large paw lands squarely on the edge of the counter, and a warm nose edges toward the platter of freshly baked scones. Bailey freezes mid-snoop, ears tilt back, as if he'd suddenly remembers the meaning of the word NO.

"Off!" as she points to the floor. "Guests first. Adorable dogs second."

Bailey's tail thumps once in defiance before he obeys, padding to his blanket in the corner of the kitchen, head down, tail still. Bailey, a mix of Springer Spaniel and German Shepherd, but one hundred percent personality, came with the Inn. Her grandmother had spoiled him rotten, and Amelia suspects he remembers every moment of it.

"Don't look at me like that," she says sternly, while she pours coffee into a carafe. "It's only fair. You got the bacon ends this morning."

With that, he plops onto his bed, his head hanging over the edge, watching those scones.

From the doorway, comes the clatter of bracelets and a voice bright enough to rival the sunlight. "If that dog ever learns to pout any harder, you'll be paying for his own therapist."

Amelia smiles without turning. "Good morning, Lila."

Lila Benson sweeps into the kitchen as though she owns it—which, in spirit, she nearly does. She lives half a mile down the road, but her daily breakfast at the Inn is as certain as sunrise. Dressed in skinny jeans, an oversized sweater the color of ripe peaches, and a scarf patterned with dancing foxes, she is the very picture of Maplewood eccentricity.

"You made the cinnamon scones again," Lila remarks while sniffing dramatically. "If you're planning to open a crime scene later, I'd like to request that these be my last meal."

"Don't start," Amelia warns, but without any edge to it.

Lila grins. "Oh, I'm not starting. I'm reminiscing. There's a difference. It's been, what, a couple of weeks since *the streamside murder*?"

Amelia groans and glances over her shoulder. "You make it sound like a novel."

"Please. Everything in Maplewood is a novel. You just have to pick the right chapter." Lila leans down to scratch Bailey's head. "Besides, the way I heard it, our brave innkeeper caught the killer right between baking muffins and walking this handsome boy here."

"I did *not* catch the killer." Amelia carries the tray of scones into the dining room. "The sheriff did. I just, helped, not like I had much of a choice."

Lila follows with two steaming carafes. "You *helped* by noticing the one detail everyone else missed. Admit it, Amelia, you've got the sleuth gene."

The dining room gleams with cozy charm—polished maple tables, hand-quilted runners, and mismatched China that somehow work together. Outside, the maples have turned from gold to copper and deep rust, their leaves skim across the porch in slow spirals. The air holds the crisp, clean chill signaling that autumn in Kansas is giving way to winter soon.

Guests filter in, smiling, still rumpled from sleep. Amelia moves from table to table with practiced ease, refilling mugs, exchanging polite chatter. She loves this rhythm—the small-town heartbeat, the sound of forks against plates, Bailey's soft nails clicking across the floorboards as he makes his rounds like an unofficial host. All the sounds combine into a perfect symphony ringing in the day ahead.

She can almost convince herself the Inn is finally running smoothly, that the dust of her grandmother's passing and the recent tragedy which had shaken Maplewood have finally settled.

Almost.

The screen door creaks, and Sheriff Tom Granger steps in. His sandy-blond hair catches the light, and his tan uniform looks freshly pressed. A faint tiredness is present in his eyes that speaks of too many late nights and too few deputies.

"Morning, Amelia," he says, the corners of his mouth lifting. "Smells like you've outdone yourself again."

Bailey bounds forward, tail wagging, double speed. Tom bends over to give him a quick pat and to ruffle his ears a bit. "Hey, buddy. Still keeping her out of trouble?"

Lila leans toward Amelia and whispers, "He's so smitten."

Amelia nearly drops the coffee pot. "He is not, Lila!"

Lila grins over her cup. She continues to whisper, "You can't tell me he doesn't come here for more than caffeine. Look at the way he's smiling. That's not professional. That's *flirtational.*"

Amelia's mouth drops open, her cheeks turn a bit rosy, and she quickly turns her head toward the window.

Tom approaches the counter in time to catch the last word. "What's flirtational?"

Amelia sets down the carafe a little too quickly. "Nothing. Lila's inventing words, again."

He gives Lila a patient smile. "That's better than inventing crimes, I suppose."

"Oh, don't tempt her," Amelia mutters.

Tom chuckles and takes a scone from the tray. "Mind if I take this on the road? Have a council meeting in twenty."

“Of course,” Amelia answers. “Oh, and here is a coffee, already in a to-go cup.”

“Thank you,” as he turns to head toward the door.

As he leaves, Lila leans her chin on her hand and sighs dramatically. “Honestly, if he ever walks in here holding a bouquet, I’ll faint from joy. For both of you.”

“Lila,” Amelia says, pouring more coffee, “you’d faint because it’d mean gossip for a month.”

Lila laughs, bright and musical. “True. But it’d be *romantic* gossip.”

The morning begins to wind down, with a gentle rhythm of clearing dishes and polite farewells, as the guests head out to start their day. Outside, the last of the guests loads luggage into the car, as the chilly wind continues to stir the maple leaves into a whispering dance. Amelia stands on the porch, waving as they drive off down the gravel lane, a faint satisfaction warms her chest.

“Peaceful,” she murmurs.

“Suspiciously peaceful,” Lila corrects her, appearing beside her with two mugs of coffee. “Which means something’s bound to happen.”

“Not every day needs to be an adventure.”

“Try telling that to Bailey.” Lila nods toward the dog, who is nose-deep in the hedge beside the walkway, tail wagging like mad. “I think he’s detecting a squirrel conspiracy.”

Amelia laughs, the sound light and genuine. Finally, Maplewood is just a sleepy town again. She takes a sip of her coffee, the warmth grounds her. They have a seat on the porch swing to enjoy the moment.

Then her phone chimes.

The cheerful trill cuts through the morning silence like a church bell. She glances down at the screen—**Dottie, Diner.**

Lila, also takes a look at the screen, raises a brow. "If she's calling instead of texting, brace yourself."

Amelia answers, while signaling Lila to be quiet. "Morning, Dottie."

The waitress's voice comes through, brisk and breathless. "Morning! It's about to be a good one! You've got a visitor coming in hot, honey. An older lady, nice hair, serious look. She said she's looking for answers, and she's heading your way right now."

"Answers to what?"

"I'll let her fill you in. But I figured you'd want the heads-up before she blows in like a Kansas storm."

Amelia's eyes roll and her head drops back, "Dottie—what does that mean?"

Too late, Dottie already hung up. Amelia looks at the phone in disbelief.

"Dottie has sent someone here, for help with something," Amelia tells Lila as she puts her phone back in her pocket.

"Help?" Lila asks. "With what?"

Bailey trots up, sitting obediently at Amelia's feet, ears perked, waiting to hear the news.

The morning breeze lifts her hair as she looks down the road... sure enough, through the trees comes the faint shape of a dusty gray sedan pulling into view.

Amelia responds after she lets out a small sigh, "I don't know, but looks like we are about to find out."

Lila sips her coffee, unbothered. "Well," she adds with cheerful finality, "looks like retirement didn't last long."

Amelia shakes her head, half-dreading, half-curious. "Maybe she just needs a place to stay."

Bailey gives a low, hopeful bark that sounds suspiciously like disagreement.

"Or," Lila suggests, eyes sparkling, "maybe she's bringing us a mystery."

Amelia rolls her eyes, but the corners of her mouth curve a bit, despite herself. "Let's hope not. Let's really, *really* hope not."

2

Woman with the Box

Gravel crunches under the tires of the older model sedan as it winds up the long lane toward the Maple Leaf Inn. Bailey barks once—deep and certain—then perches himself at the top of the porch stairs.

"That must be she," Lila says.

"Dottie said 'older lady with a serious face,' so she sure looks like our visitor," Amelia observes. "Let's not assume she's here about anything dramatic. Maybe she's just a soon-to-be guest."

"Guests don't drive with that kind of determination," Lila replies. "That's a woman with *purpose*. Possibly vengeance."

"*Lila*."

"All right, fine. Purpose and luggage."

Amelia stands up and waves as the woman in her early seventies, neatly dressed in a wool coat, exits the car. Then she opens the back door and pulls out a worn cardboard box and holds it close to her chest with one hand as she shuts the door with the other. She looks toward the Inn, her eyes appear tired, deeper than a sleepy tired.

"Miss Hartford?"

"Yes," Amelia replies. "Please, come on in, out of the cold." Amelia, opens the door and holds it open, guiding the women forward with her hand, as Bailey moves over to let her pass.

"Thank you, I am Edna Hampton." As Edna approaches the door, she seems to be sizing Amelia up. "Dottie mentioned you were in your early thirties, long brown hair, often pulled back, and you had a warm welcoming smile." Edna's face softens a bit, "And it seems she described you well, plus your furry companion too."

Amelia smiles as Edna passes her.

She steps inside, pausing a few steps down the hall, allowing the others to come in after.

The warmth of the Inn seems to ease some invisible tension from her shoulders.

"Please go straight ahead to the kitchen, we can sit down and I will get us some coffee," Amelia offers.

Once in the kitchen, Bailey circles Edna once, nose twitching, then sits neatly at her feet offering a welcome.

Edna smiles faintly. "Well, aren't you handsome? My husband and I used to have a Shepherd mix. Loyal as the day is long." Edna pauses and looks down at Bailey. "May I set this on the table," gesturing to the box, "and pet your lovely friend?"

"Of course. He was my grandmother's dog," Amelia explains, "I inherited both the Inn and Bailey." Amelia heads over to the counter to prepare coffee.

Edna sets the box on the table, and then bends over a bit to give Bailey a proper petting.

Lila leans casually against the banister. "Lucky you. Two things that attract trouble and company."

Amelia turns back to give Lila a look, then back to Edna, "This is Lila Benson, my neighbor and..."

Lila interrupts brightly, "Her unpaid assistant, consultant, and comic relief." Lila nods. "Nice to meet you."

Edna's polite smile deepened a fraction. "It's a pleasure to meet you both."

Amelia motions toward the table. "Please, have a seat. Would you like tea? Coffee?"

"Coffee, black, would be wonderful, thank you," Edna replies as she takes a seat. Bailey sits down too, right next to her.

The nearby parlor's fire pops softly in the background. The smell of the burning wood and the cinnamon still hanging in the air from the morning's scones, creates a soothing mood. Amelia's puts a fresh cup of coffee down for Edna and then heads back to the counter to refill her cup, but Lila is already on it, handing Amelia her cup. Their eyes keep drifting to the box resting on the table in front of Edna, wondering if it is something precious or dangerous.

Edna breaks the silence, "I should start by thanking you for seeing me," resting one hand on the box. "I wasn't sure how to approach this. Dottie, at the diner, said you might be willing to listen or even help me out."

Amelia smiles faintly. "Dottie tends to volunteer me for things routinely."

"She said you helped the sheriff with that awful business by the stream," Edna says quietly. "The story in the paper."

Amelia hesitates, taking another drink of her coffee, "I didn't do much. Just... noticed a few details."

Lila arches a brow. "She's being modest. Amelia's practically Maplewood's Miss Marple."

Amelia shoots her another look. "Without the knitting, of course," Lila clarifies.

Edna's lips twitch into the faintest smile, then her gaze falls back to the box. "My son, Eric, died here ten years ago. They said it was a hunting accident, clean and simple. Sheriff Hank Ross handled the case. I live in Colorado. It was the sheriff who called, told me my boy tripped and his gun went off. They sent me his things, a while later, including this box. You know, his personal effects."

Her voice grows quieter. "My husband was very sick at the time, fighting cancer. I couldn't deal with more grief, so I put the boxes away in the garage without opening them."

Amelia exchanges a glance with Lila, who for once doesn't say a word.

Edna stares into her coffee for a moment, then goes on. "Eric was our only child. Smart when he wanted to be, funny too, but restless. He got into trouble a lot as a teenager—petty stuff at first. Fights, driving without a license, skipping school. His father thought hard work would straighten him out, but Eric just wanted to be somewhere else. After he graduated, he packed a duffel bag and left without telling us where he was going. We didn't hear from him again."

Amelia, reaches over to the counter and grabs a tissue, holding it out to Edna.

Edna, nods as she takes the tissue, pauses, swallows hard. "I used to wait for the phone to ring, thinking he'd call to say he'd found a good job or met someone nice. Instead, one night, the sheriff here called. Told me my boy was dead. Said he'd been living in Maplewood for a while. I didn't even know that."

Amelia reaches out to place her hand on Edna's. "I am so sorry for your loss, I cannot imagine the pain you have been carrying around with you."

Edna places her other hand, trembling slightly, over Amelia's, "Thank you, dear. I so appreciate you letting me talk with you about all this." She uses the tissue to wipe away a tear. "A couple years ago, my husband passed away. Shortly after that, I finally found the courage to open the boxes."

Lila adds, "I am sure that was tough, unpacking his past."

"It was," Edna explains, "but there were things inside that made me doubt the story I was told. And a letter that made me think he knew something was coming, something that wasn't an accident."

Amelia's throat tightens. "That must have been hard to read."

"Yes," Edna says softly as she nodded slowly. "But it is harder to keep wondering."

The room falls quiet except for the low hiss of the fire. Outside, a gust of late-autumn wind rattles the windowpanes. Bailey lifts his paw and rests it on Edna's knee, she grins down at him and gives him a loving stroke down his head.

Lila leans forward. "So, you think someone here in town might've done him harm?"

"I don't know," Edna admits. "But I think someone knows more than they ever said. And I intend to find out."

Amelia sits back, fingers drumming against her coffee cup. "Have you spoke with Sheriff Granger about this?"

"Yes. I called him early this morning. He was kind. Said he'd look into the records and see what was there. He wasn't here back then, so he personally doesn't know anything about my son's death."

Amelia frowns. "So, he hasn't actually looked yet?"

Lila chimes in, "Not likely, he had that meeting this morning, remember?"

"No, I haven't heard from him since we spoke this morning. I'm sure it's not a priority," Edna sighs as she lowers her gaze. Edna reaches out, her hand trembling slightly as she lays it over Amelia's. "I'm not asking for a miracle. I only need someone who'll really see what's in front of them."

"Come on," Lila encourages, almost on the edge of her chair, "You've already got the instincts. And she's come all this way."

"*Lila*," Amelia warns.

Bailey gives a low, sympathetic whine and rests his chin on Edna's knee.

Amelia exhales slowly, her resolve softens. "All right. We'll take a look together. No promises, but I'll help however I can."

Edna's shoulders drop with visible relief. "Thank you, Miss Hartford. You have no idea what this means."

Lila grins. "You've done it again, Amelia. Hooked another mystery before lunch."

Amelia gives her a look, but isn't able to hold back a small smile of her own. "Mrs. Hampton, why don't you stay for a bite to eat before you leave? Lila's always right about one thing—investigating's easier on a full stomach."

"Call me Edna," she says, smiling easier now. "And thank you. I didn't realize how hungry I am."

Bailey's tail starts wagging and he scurries to his bowls; he knows what "hungry" means.

They share soup and sandwiches while Bailey stations himself under the table in hopeful anticipation. Between bites, Edna tells small stories about Eric as a boy—how he'd once rescued a stray cat and hidden it in his closet, how he'd charm his teachers and then skip class the next day. Her pride and sorrow twined together in every word. Then, she fills in the details of his arrests for theft and assaults, as well as the suspicions in their hometown about his other shady dealings.

"You know, when we were living through all that, there were times I wished he would get caught and be locked up," Edna confesses. "It was so hard and nothing we did to try and get him on the straight and narrow worked."

"I just wish I'd known what happened in those years after he left," she says softly. "Maybe I could have helped. Maybe he wouldn't have ended up here."

Amelia shakes her head gently. "You did what any mother would do. Sometimes people have to walk into their own storms."

Lila dabs her mouth with a napkin. "And sometimes storms have a habit of circling back to town. Good thing we've got umbrellas."

Amelia chuckles, the sound breaking the heaviness for a moment.

They all get up and clear the table. Edna returns to the table, sets her hand on the box, "If you don't mind, I'd like to come back after I rest for a bit. Maybe mid-afternoon? We could look inside together, then."

"Of course," Amelia said. "We'll keep it safe."

"Thank you and also for the delicious lunch and your ears," Edna takes her coat from the rack and bundles back up.

As Edna heads for the door, Bailey escorts her with solemn dignity, tail swaying slow back and forth in cadence with their steps.

Once the sedan disappears down the lane, Lila rests her weight against the counter and exhales. "Well, that settles it. You're in."

"I said I'd *look*," Amelia corrects her.

Lila winks. "Which in your language means 'prepare the evidence board.'"

Bailey barks once, agreeing.

Amelia shakes her head, glancing at the box now sitting under the soft light of the kitchen window. "I need to get things cleaned up."

3

A Box of Secrets

By midafternoon, a thin constant drizzle develops over Maplewood, painting the Inn's windows with silver streaks. The air smells faintly of rain and woodsmoke, and the quiet murmur of Bailey's snoring fills the parlor.

Amelia straightens the quilt on the sofa for the third time, trying not to admit she's waiting for Edna's car to reappear up the lane. As she works, she keeps thinking about what could be in the box. Asking herself, is it possible to get answers for Edna ten years after the fact?

"You're pretending to tidy," Lila calls out from her perch by the window. "But what you're really doing is pacing in disguise."

"I'm not pacing," Amelia insists.

"You're moving in circles and adjusting furniture that doesn't need adjusting. Classic pre-mystery behavior."

Bailey lifts his head at the sound of Lila's voice, then yawns wide enough to show all his teeth, then lays back down.

Amelia crosses her arms. "You could go home, you know. No one's forcing you to be here."

Lila giggles, "Please, I wouldn't miss the grand unveiling. It's not every day someone shows up with a box of secrets."

Before Amelia can reply, the familiar crunch of tires on gravel reaches their ears. Bailey pops up in an instant and trots toward the door, his tail swinging with excitement.

"Showtime," Lila nearly cheers.

Amelia opens the door to find Edna on the porch, a scarf tied around her head. The drizzle has dotted her coat with darker patches, but her eyes look brighter, more hopeful, than they were this morning.

"Come in before you catch cold," Amelia says, ushering her inside.

Edna steps into the fire-warmed air of the parlor and unbuttons her coat. "I hope I'm not too early," she says, glancing toward the kitchen. "I haven't been able to stop thinking about the box."

"You're right on time," admits Amelia with a reassuring smile. "It's been sitting on the kitchen table waiting for you."

"And calling to us like a siren," Lila adds, already heading that way.

Bailey follows with a happy bounce in his step, nails clicking on the old wood floor. The scent of the cinnamon candles that Amelia lit earlier near the window fill the kitchen now. A sharp whistle from the tea kettle sounds off. "Oh, I forgot! I put on water for some hot tea," Amelia explains as she rushes to the stove to turn off the burner.

"That sounds wonderful," Edna replies as she takes a seat at the table.

Lila chimes in, "Yes it does," as she heads to the cabinet to get them all cups.

Amelia has the tea steeping in a beautiful China teapot, with intricate pink flowers hand painted all over it. She places on the table and announces, "It'll be ready in a few minutes."

The three women now gather around the table where the weathered box sits beneath the warm glow of the overhead light. Its corners now softened by age, remnants of the tape, now brittle, still remain on the sides.

Edna rests her hands on the lid for a long moment before lifting it open. "I've already been through everything in here," she admits. "But saying it out loud, showing someone else, is making it all feel new again. I suppose I really need to see if someone else can see what I see."

"And we're here for exactly that," Amelia reassures her.

Lila clasps her hands together dramatically. "Ladies and gentleman—well, ladies and dog—the moment we've all been waiting for."

Bailey barks twice, confirming the excitement.

Edna smiles faintly, pats Bailey's head and then opens the box. "These are the things I picked out which I felt would be helpful." She removes the items with care, laying each on the table.

The collection forms in front of them: a hunter's safety certificate, a gun club membership card, a small brass key engraved with 312, an old photograph, a manilla envelope, and an old worn paperback copy of *The Picture of Dorian Gray*.

They all lean closer.

"Well," Lila says softly. "These are definitely secrets, is that all we have to go on?"

Edna picks up the hunter's certificate and the gun club card, as she smooths them gently with her fingertips. "These were his," she explains. "I called the club. They knew him. They said he always followed safety protocols and practiced at the range regularly." She pauses and then continues. "But the sheriff said he died in a hunting accident, I just can't make sense of it. He'd gone to all that trouble to get certified, to practice, I kept wondering... how could someone who took it that seriously... make a mistake like that?"

Amelia places her hand on Edna's arm, "So you brought the things that didn't fit or make sense to you?"

Edna nods. "Exactly. The rest was just clothes and old papers. These were the pieces that wouldn't let me sleep."

Lila murmurs, "The things that whisper to you, until you listen."

Amelia nods slowly, while in thought, her eyes moving to the small brass key. She picks it up, turning it over in her palm. "This key, it looks like a safe-deposit key."

Lila in excitement, "Perfect, we only have one bank in town..."

"Maplewood Bank," Amelia finishes, nodding.

Edna frowns. "That was my thought too. But I went to that bank, when I was here ten years ago to take his body home, I closed his bank account, they never said anything about him having a safe deposit box."

"We'll figure it out," Amelia promises.

Amelia picks up the book, the spine is creased from long-ago handling: *The Picture of Dorian Gray*. Amelia opens it carefully, pages whispering as she turns through the yellowed pages. "Does this book hold some significance?"

Edna answers, "I don't think so, I was surprised a book was in his things, Eric always hated to read."

Amelia keeps flipping through it until she finds something folded neatly in the middle of the book. A single page of lined notebook paper. The paper appears to have been wadded up or folded in multiple ways, but the handwriting is still legible.

Edna takes in a deep breath, "That's it," she whispers. "That's the letter Eric left me—I found it folded up in that book. I assumed he had used the book to hide it."

Lila leans in, "Okay to read it out loud?"

Amelia hesitates, glancing at Edna for permission.

"Please," Edna urges softly.

Amelia smooths the paper on the table and begins.

Mom,

I don't even know where to start. I've wanted to come home a hundred times, but every time I thought about it, I saw the look Dad would give me. The one that says he's done bailing me out. I know I've disappointed you both more than once, and this time, well, this time I've made a real mess.

I'm working for people I shouldn't be. Thought it would be easy money, just a few runs back and forth, but it's more than that now. I don't think I can just walk away, but I have to try. If anything happens to me, please don't believe I meant for it to.

I can't go to the sheriff, he's too close to the wrong people, and I don't know who's really on whose side. I have to sort this out myself. I just want to make things right before it's too late.

Tell Dad I was trying. I know I don't deserve another chance, but I'm still your son. Maybe I can fix one thing before I'm gone.

Love, Eric

As Amelia finishes, the only sound in the room is the low crackle of the fire. Edna's hands twisting a tissue, which she lifts to dry the tears as they come.

"Oh, Eric..." she whispers.

Lila breaks the silence first, her voice soft. "He sounds like a man who knew he was in deep trouble."

Edna nods, eyes glimmering from the tears. "He was never good at hiding things from me, even when he was a boy. I can almost hear his voice in those words."

Amelia folds the letter carefully, returns it to the book. "This doesn't prove anything yet," she says gently, "but it tells us he was afraid to trust law enforcement back then. That might be why the original investigation was handled so quickly."

Lila leans back, crossing her arms. "Well, if we're talking about the sheriff from back then—Hank Ross—no surprise there. My mother always said he had a temper you could set your watch by. Big fish in a small pond, and he liked to remind folks of it. Wouldn't shock me one bit if he wasn't half as honest as he pretended."

"*Lila,*" Amelia warns softly, though she didn't disagree.

"What?" Lila shrugs. "You can't live in Maplewood without hearing things. And I've got two good ears."

Amelia tries to smile but can't quite manage it. Her thoughts are already turning over, one by one. Eric's letter. The photograph. The key. The faint mention of a sheriff too close to the wrong people. It is too much coincidence to ignore—but too little proof to accuse.

Still, a small voice inside her whispers that this isn't something she can just leave alone.

Lila interrupts her thought, "Hey what about this picture? That's Hank in the middle, who's he with?" She holds up the photo, of three men standing together, dressed in camo, with bright orange hats and vests, each with a shotgun.

"The one on the left is Eric, I don't know who the other man is," Edna explains.

Lila adds, "Well I would say old Hank knew your son pretty well if they went out hunting together."

"Okay, at this point, I think," Amelia, chimes in, her tone careful, "the next step is to visit Sheriff Granger. See what's in the old file, then we will have a better idea of how solid the accidental death finding was or maybe even find some information in the file that will point us somewhere else."

Edna sighs with relief. "You think he'll talk to me?"

"I think he'll listen," Amelia explains. "He's a good man. And he won't mind if I stop by with you."

Lila arches a brow. "Oh, he won't mind at all," she mutters under her breath.

Amelia ignores her, already reaching for her phone. She hesitates a second before pressing Tom's contact, her thumb hovering just long enough for Lila to notice and grin.

When he answers, his voice was warm but alert. "Afternoon, Amelia. Everything all right?"

"Yes," she replies, glancing at Edna. "I just... there's something I'd like to talk to you about. Nothing urgent, but it is important."

"All right," Tom agrees, after a pause. "I've got a few reports to finish tonight, but if you want to stop by tomorrow morning, say around ten, I'll make sure I'm free."

"That's perfect, Thank you."

A brief silence, before he replies, "Anytime, Amelia. See you in the morning."

"Yes, see you at ten." She ends the call.

Edna exhales slowly, a soft smile emerges.

"Then it's settled," Amelia says. "We'll go see Sheriff Granger after breakfast."

Bailey gives a single thump of his tail against the floor, as if agreeing the investigation has officially began.

"Amelia, I cannot thank you enough for listening and agreeing to help me, most of all, for not thinking I am crazy," Edna says as she stands and heads to her coat. "I am going back to the motel, I feel like I can actually get a good night's sleep tonight."

Amelia walks with her to the door. "Yes, you get some sleep and we will pick this up in the morning." She holds the door as Edna leaves for the night, and Lila is right behind her.

"Me too, I will be back for breakfast," Lila says as she walks out the door, then turns, "Don't stay up all night mulling all the pieces over."

Amelia smiles and waves her off.

4

Accidental Death

The morning dawns crisp and clear, sunlight glinting off the damp leaves still hanging on the maple trees lining Maplewood's main street. The clouds from yesterday have all floated away, making for a bright sunny new day. Amelia parks the car outside the Sheriff's Office, Bailey's nose presses against the window, pleading to go too.

"Sorry, detective," Amelia says, as she reaches to the back seat and pats his head. "You're sitting this one out."

Bailey whines softly, fogging the glass with his breath.

Lila and Edna are already waiting near the front steps, bundled in scarves against the cool wind. Lila's scarf today is a bold swirl of red and gold, entirely too bright for official business, but perfect for her.

"Morning," Amelia calls out, as she closes the car door and heads toward them.

"Morning," Edna replies, clutching her handbag. A nervous energy in the older woman's eyes, perhaps a fragile mix of hope and fear that Amelia recognizes too well.

Lila reassures her, "He's not as scary as he looks, you know. The sheriff, I mean. The last one was a different story, but Tom's one of the good ones. Plus, he has great coffee."

Amelia joins them, as they are about to head in. "Remember, we're not mentioning the box or anything in it. The key, the photo, the letter—none of that. We just want to see what's in the official file. If the case is closed, we don't have enough to warrant re-opening it."

Lila makes a show of zipping her lips. "Scout's honor," she promises. "Besides, there's no reason to hand things over to collect more dust."

"You were never a scout," Amelia muttered, "but you're right."

"Actually, I was for a week," Lila adds brightly. "Got a badge in creative thinking."

Edna manages a smile, she just can't help herself. "Okay, I am ready."

The three women step through the glass door into the Sheriff's Office. The scent of paper, coffee, and faint disinfectant fill the air. A bulletin board on one wall is tacked full of lost dog notices, bake-sale flyers, and one poster about seat-belt safety that looks older than Amelia herself.

Behind the counter, a young man looks up from a stack of reports. Deputy Alex Ruiz—Amelia remembers him from the last case. He has neatly combed dark hair and the air of a young man balancing ten tasks at once.

He smiles politely. “Good morning, Miss. Hartford.” His gaze shifts to Edna. “And you are?”

Amelia steps aside. “This is Mrs. Edna Hampton.”

Edna extends her hand. “Nice to meet you, Deputy.”

Ruiz shook it warmly. “Likewise. The Sheriff's in his office. You can head right in.” The Deputy turns to Lila. “Oh, good morning to you as well, Lila.”

Lila gives him a wave and a smile as they pass.

Inside, Sheriff Tom Granger is leaning over his desk, phone wedged between his shoulder and ear, scribbling something on a yellow notepad. When he looks up and sees them, his face breaks into an easy smile that softens the rugged lines around his eyes.

He ends the call and motions them in. “Well, this is a surprise. I was expecting maybe a broken fence complaint or Bailey's latest escapade, not a whole committee.”

Lila grins, “We only travel in groups, it confuses the gossips.”

Tom chuckles, then glances to Edna, “I don't think we've met.”

Edna takes a small step forward, her voice steady but gentle. “We spoke on the phone, early yesterday morning, about my son, Eric Hampton. He died here about ten years ago. You were kind enough to agree to check the records.”

Recognition flickers across Tom's face, and his smile fades into something more solemn. "Yes, I remember that call. I'm very sorry for your loss, Mrs. Hampton."

"Thank you," she replies softly. "I've come back hoping to… understand it better."

Tom's gaze moves to Amelia, one eye raises, "And how do you fit into this mission?"

Amelia smiles lightly but keeps her tone calm. "Mrs. Hampton came to visit the Inn. We got to talking, and it seems only fair she has someone local to go with her. She's driven ten hours from Colorado looking for answers, for some closure. If there's a file on the case, maybe simply reviewing it might help her find some peace."

Tom sits down in his chair, while extending his hand to the ladies, to choose a seat too. As he studies Amelia, "So, you want me to pull a closed file?"

"Just to look," she offers. "No trouble, no paperwork. You'd still have all the authority, she needs to know what's there, if she was told everything…"

Lila adds sweetly, "And what's not there. Because something about this whole 'accidental death' feels about as tidy as a pigsty."

"*Lila*," Amelia mutters as she gently elbows her.

Tom sighs, gets up, rubbing the back of his neck. "You're lucky I'm a patient man." He walks toward the hallway as he calls out, "Ruiz, hey, can you check the archives for a file on Eric Hampton? Should be around ten years back, marked accidental death under Sheriff Hank Ross."

Ruiz nods and disappears into the back room.

While they wait, Tom pours coffee into mismatched mugs. As he passes them each a coffee, "Mrs. Hampton, I do have to apologize, I have not checked the case myself, yet. But since you are here, with reinforcements, there's no harm in reviewing what's already public record, together."

"Thank you, sheriff, I really do appreciate you taking the time to do this," Edna says.

"But, just so we're clear," Tom begins to explain. "I can't officially reopen anything without cause," as his stare moves from Edna to Amelia by the end of the sentence.

Amelia's eyes meet his, she flashes a small, grateful smile. "That's all we're asking, a look."

A few minutes later, Ruiz returns carrying a thin brown folder, that appears empty at first glance, "This is it," as he hands it to Tom, "I double checked to make sure there wasn't another file."

"That's comforting," as Lila rolls her eyes dramatically.

Tom opens the file on his desk. The pages inside are sparse. Amelia leans slightly forward, curiosity sharpening her focus.

At the top of the first page: *Accident Report – Eric Hampton – October 17, 2015.*

The report is brief. *A single victim found, male mid-to-late 20s, one mile into wooded area off County Road 6. Apparent shotgun wound, upper torso. Found with a shotgun near body, no signs of a struggle. Body was reported by two out of towners who had been hiking through the woods. They reported he had no pulse when they found him. They did not report hearing the shot or seeing anyone else in the area.*

Attached was a single photograph: a man's body lying near a shotgun, fallen leaves scattered around him.

The signature at the bottom was Hank's.

Edna attempts to speak, but the words won't come. Amelia rests a steadying hand on her arm.

"I've seen this photo," Edna says softly. "They sent me a copy with his belongings."

Tom flips to the next page, his brows knitting. "This is the death certificate, signed by old Doc Brown, certifying the cause of death as an accidental shooting." Tom turns to his Deputy. "Ruiz, do you know if Doc Brown was ever the coroner here?"

"Not that I know, let me go check the computer records and see who it was in October 2015, just to be sure," as Ruiz heads to his desk.

"That's all that's here, no witness statements or coroner's report. No ballistics workup. Just this single summary, handwritten and signed by Hank Ross. Not even a serial-number was recorded for the gun pictured." Tom shakes his head and then rests his forehead in the palm of his hand as Ruiz re-enters the room.

Ruiz leans over and softly tells Tom, "No record of Doc Brown being a coroner. Back then it was Dr. William Henderson. I think he moved out of state a couple years back. Also, I checked and there is no chain-of-custody log entry. Was the gun even collected as evidence?"

"Doesn't say." Tom frowns deeper. "We'd normally have at least a coroner's summary and some lab data."

Lila crosses her arms. "So basically, Hank wrote 'oops, accident' and called it good?"

Tom shoots her a look somewhere between exasperation and amusement. "Something like that."

He closes the file. "No inventory sheet, no mention of returning personal items to family. That's it, other than the CASE CLOSED sticker on the outside."

Edna's voice trembles slightly, as she asks, "Really, that's all there is?"

"For now," Tom answers. "But I can check with county records and the coroner's office, they keep records too, perhaps we can find something there. If the information is just missing, it might still exist somewhere. I'll do some digging."

Amelia's brows knit together. "It seems awfully thin, doesn't it? Especially for a death involving a firearm."

Tom nods. "You're right. There should be more here. At minimum, a coroner's report, lab test results, and ballistics or something on the gun. I'll make a few calls later today."

Edna exhales slowly. "Thank you, Sheriff. I know it's been years. I just... need to know the truth, whatever it is."

Tom's tone calms. "You deserve that. I'll do what I can, but until something concrete turns up, it's still officially an accidental death."

Ruiz picked up the file. "I'll scan and copy everything so Mrs. Hampton can keep a copy."

Tom nods, as he adds, "And, Ruiz, go ahead and reach out to the county coroner's office. See what they've got from ten years back."

As the deputy leaves, the Sheriff turns back to Edna. "I wish I could promise answers, but these old cases can be tricky. Still, I'll give it a fair look."

Edna manages a small, weary smile, "That's more than I've had in ten years."

"Then it's a start," Tom says kindly. "Remember, officially the case is closed. Without new evidence I can't reopen it."

Edna nods.

"But if you happen to notice something... I wouldn't stop you from bringing it to me," Tom adds.

Lila elbows Amelia without anyone noticing, except Amelia, who rolls her eyes.

Outside, the autumn sunlight has warmed the sidewalk though the air still carries a cool bite. Edna looks pale but composed, her hand grips her purse strap tightly.

Amelia rests a hand on her shoulder. "Let's get you back to your motel for now. He's going to do his part. We'll do ours."

Edna nods, "You've already done more than I expected."

"You'd be surprised how much trouble she can get into in one morning," Lila adds, looping her arm through Amelia's and giving it a hug.

That draws a faint laugh from Edna, the first Amelia's heard from her all day.

Together they watch and wave as Edna climbs into her car and drives off toward the Maplewood Motel.

For a long moment, Amelia stands on the sidewalk, the morning breeze teasing at the loose strands of her hair. Down the street, the sign for the Bakery creaks softly in the wind.

Part of her wants to leave it, to trust that Tom will find what he can and that will be enough. He'll probably lecture her again about "staying out of official matters." And maybe he'll be right.

But something about that thin, all but empty file won't let her go. It isn't simply the lack of answers; it is more about what *wasn't* included, intentionally. Reports missing. Evidence unlisted. A life summed up in half a page.

Her grandmother's words drift through her mind, clear as if she was standing right next to her, speaking: *We should always do what we can to help others in need.*

The motto her grandmother had lived by and the fire that built the Maple Leaf Inn into a refuge for anyone who crossed its porch.

Amelia takes a slow breath. "All right, Grandma," she murmurs under her breath, "message received."

When she turns back to Lila, her decision is already made.

Lila tilts her head, reading her expression perfectly. "So," she says, drawing out the word, "where do we start?"

Amelia looks back toward the Sheriff's Office, then down the quiet street where the red and gold leaves skitter across the pavement.

"Where it all began," she replies softly. "At the beginning."

Lila grins. "Now that's the spirit."

5

Echoes of the Past

The courthouse clock strikes eleven as Amelia and Lila stand on the sidewalk in front of the Sheriff's office. The sunlight has sharpened since they left the Inn, and is bright enough now to make the wet pavement glisten.

Lila exhales loudly. "Well. That was about as satisfying as decaf."

Amelia smiles faintly. "You mean the missing reports, the nonexistent evidence, or the part where the Sheriff who filed it all, happened to retire right after?"

"All of the above," Lila agrees, tugging her scarf tighter. "You know what this means, right?"

"That I'm going to regret getting involved again?"

"That *we're* getting involved again," Lila corrects her, pointing toward the street. "Starting now. But first, we need our secret weapon."

"Bailey," Amelia confirms, already nodding.

"Exactly. No offense, but I trust that dog's instincts more than half the men in this county."

Amelia laughs softly, shaking her head. "You are in luck, he is asleep in the back seat, insisted on coming. But let's swing by the Inn, drop your car off, feed Bailey his lunch, then take my car to the diner. We can grab our lunch and... start talking strategy."

"Or gossip," Lila said, following her to the car. "Strategy sounds so formal."

The two cars turn onto the gravel drive of the Maple Leaf Inn a few minutes later. Amelia parks by the porch while Lila pulls off to the side behind her. Bailey's eagerness gets the best of him, as he plasters his face against the window watching Lila get out.

"See?" Lila says. "He knows it's time."

Amelia opens the back door and Bailey bounds toward Lila, tail wagging so hard his entire back half wiggles with joy. Lila is ready for him, greeting him a hug and some strokes.

"Okay, boy, let's get you some food," Amelia promises as they head inside.

Bailey rushes straight for his bowls and sits to wait patient-ly.

Lila giggles at him, "He has the hurry-up-and-wait down to a science."

"So true." Amelia gives him a pat on the head and pours his food into the bowl. "Oh, I forgot to ask you, how is your new book coming?"

"I can't believe I forgot to tell you, I finished it," as a smile stretches across Lila's face. "I sent it to the editor yesterday and I should have proofs for the cover in the next few days."

"That is great news. I am so happy for you. I can't wait to see it."

"I won't forget to show you, promise."

"Okay, detective Bailey," Amelia announces as he finishes up. "You're officially on duty."

"Underpaid and overqualified," Lila quips, following close behind.

They pile into Amelia's car, Bailey hops proudly into the back seat like a true canine deputy.

As they cruise down Main Street toward the diner, the familiar rhythm of their friendship returns—half banter, half brainstorming.

"You realize," Lila says, "we're turning into those people. You know, the ones who can't leave a mystery alone."

Amelia keeps her eyes on the road, the corners of her mouth curving. "I'm pretty sure you were born that way."

"True, but you weren't. You're the responsible one. The adult. The voice of reason."

Amelia arches a brow. "Is that what you think?"

"That's what you used to be," Lila clarifies. "Then, you got a taste for intrigue and potential danger."

"Hardly," Amelia quickly gives her the look. "I just can't stand it when something doesn't add up. That file today," she shakes her head. "It felt wrong. Like someone had gone out of their way to leave nothing behind."

As she finishes the sentence, it carries her mind back to her years as a law clerk in the city. She learned then that patterns told the truth long before people did. When something didn't line up, a missing signature, an unexplained expense, usually meant someone wanted it that way.

"Exactly," Lila blurts out, breaking her thoughts. "Which means it's time for some good old-fashioned fieldwork. Dottie's bound to know something. She always does."

"Dottie's gossip is ninety percent exaggeration."

"Which means ten percent fact," Lila counters. "And we only need the ten."

Bailey lets out a small bark from the back seat, as if agreeing.

Amelia glances at him in the rearview mirror, her resolve tightening. "All right then," she says. "Lunch and information gathering."

"And pie," Lila adds. "You can't interrogate anyone on an empty stomach."

Amelia laughs softly as she turns into the diner's small parking lot. "You really should put that on a bumper sticker."

The familiar neon sign of *Dottie's Diner* buzzes faintly in the midday light, the red paint of the door faded from years of Kansas sun. Inside, the air is thick with the smell of coffee, fried chicken, and the sweet tang of Dottie's famous peach cobbler.

Dottie herself is behind the counter, refilling mugs with her usual efficiency. Her gray hair tucked into a bun, a pencil lodged firmly behind one ear. She looks up and her face breaks into a smile.

"Well, if it isn't my favorite troublemakers," she hollers out, setting down the coffee pot. "And Bailey too. Lord, that dog's gotten bigger."

"More dignified," Lila corrects. "He's an investigator now. He sniffs out lies."

Dottie snorts before she can speak. "In this town, he's going to need a bigger nose."

They pick a booth near the window, and Dottie arrives a moment later with a fresh pot of coffee for Lila and Amelia and a bowl of water for Bailey. Bailey slurps it all up and then curls up under the table, tail occasionally thumping against Amelia's shoes.

"So," Dottie starts, resting one hand on her hip. "You here to tell me you're back on the case, or should I guess?"

Amelia lifts her brows. "Word travels fast."

"In Maplewood? Honey, it travels faster than the mail truck," says Dottie with a wink. "Mrs. Hampton came in this morning. Looked like she'd seen a ghost. She mentioned she was headed your way. I'm glad she hooked up with you."

"She did," Amelia replies carefully. "We just met with the Sheriff about her son's death."

Dottie's smile fades, her eyes soften. "Poor woman. I remember when that happened. Hunting accident, they said. But..." She shook her head. "Eric was always a careful boy. Too careful, for that kind of mistake."

Lila leans forward. "What else do you remember about him?"

Dottie glances around, making sure no one else is close enough to hear. "Quiet kid. Kept to himself mostly. Lived with his mama until he took off after high school. I think he worked odd jobs around town when he got here, helped at the hardware store, maybe at the gas station for a bit."

Amelia takes a sip of her coffee. "Did he have any close friends?"

"I only recall maybe Jimmy Dale. The two of them were thick as thieves for a while." Dottie frowns thoughtfully. "Then one day, Jimmy's around alone, no Eric with him."

"Did he ever say anything about why Eric was gone?" Amelia questions.

"He did mention he thought Eric was in some kind of trouble, but he didn't give any details. You know, Jimmy's always been the dependable one. If something needs fixing, he's the man everyone goes to, probably why Eric befriended him."

Lila's eyes sparkle. "Trouble, you say? The good kind or the bad kind?"

Dottie raises an eyebrow. "You tell me, Miss Writer. The kind where the Sheriff starts asking questions, then stops suddenly like someone told him to."

Amelia's head tilts slightly. "Someone told him to?"

"Can't prove it," Dottie admits, lowering her voice. "But Hank Ross was running the department then, and if there's one thing I learned about Hank, it's that he liked things neat and quiet. Especially when they weren't."

A shadow passes over Amelia's expression. She remembers Hank Ross vaguely from her grandmother's time. Gruff, self-important, the sort of man who treated authority as a personal inheritance.

Before she can reply, the bell over the door jingles.

Mayor Charles Tuttle steps in, his pressed suit slightly at odds with the diner's checkered floors. He makes his usual slow, assessing sweep of the room before his gaze lands on Amelia's booth.

"Well, well," he mocks, walking over. "Our local celebrity and her entourage."

"Good afternoon, Mayor," Amelia replies.

"Ladies." He nods curtly to Lila and Dottie, then leans one hand on the edge of the booth. "I hear Mrs. Hampton's in town asking questions about her son's death."

"News really does travel fast," Lila murmurs.

Tuttle ignores her. "I'd be careful about getting mixed up in that business again, Miss Hartford. This town's had enough excitement for one year."

"Mrs. Hampton needs answers and closure," Amelia explains. "That doesn't sound dangerous."

He straightens, his tone sharpening. "Closure's one thing. Digging into old wounds is another. Let the Sheriff handle it."

Dottie wipes down the counter a little more forcefully than necessary. "Letting the Sheriff handle it is what we did last time, Charles. Look how that turned out."

Tuttle's jaw tightens, but he doesn't reply. After a beat, he nods stiffly and heads for the register, orders a coffee to go.

The moment he leaves, Lila exhales. "I swear, if that man had his way, we'd all be living in some kind of Stepford version of Maplewood."

Dottie smirks. "He just doesn't like surprises. Or women with opinions."

"Then he must *love* us," Lila says, reaching for the sugar packets.

Amelia smiles faintly but her attention drifts toward the front door, where Bailey is standing now, head and ears at attention. A second later, the bell above the door jingles again.

A man stands at the doorway, hood pulled low, shoulders hunched. He peers inside just long enough for Amelia to catch a glimpse of sharp eyes and a jagged scar near his temple. Bailey lets out a low, warning growl.

Then, as quickly as he appeared, he turns and disappears down the street.

Every conversation in the diner pauses for a heartbeat. Dottie looks toward the door, frowning. "That's strange. I didn't recognize him."

"Neither did I," as Amelia follows the direction the man went.

Lila leans down, calls Bailey back over to the table and scratches his head. "That's Bailey's suspect radar," she whispers. "Never wrong."

Amelia nods slowly. As she contemplates for a moment about the scar and the quickness of his retreat. It wasn't just someone curious. He was looking for someone.

She drops a few bills on the table and stands. "Come on. I think it's time we head back to the Inn."

Lila blinks and glares at Amelia. "Already? We just got pie."

"You can take it to go," Amelia says while slipping her coat on. "If we're going to help Edna, we need to start with what she left us. The box, the photo, the letter, all of it."

Lila brightens right up, grabbing her half-eaten slice of peach cobbler and scooping it into a napkin. "Finally. The part where we turn into sleuths again."

Dottie crosses her arms. "You two be careful. That woman's already been through enough without you stirring up more ghosts."

"We'll be careful," Amelia promises.

Bailey gives another low rumble, eyes still fixed on the door as if he can sense the lingering trace of whoever had been present.

As they step back into the crisp afternoon light, Amelia glances once down the street. The man is gone, but unease curls low in her stomach.

The autumn air is still cold while the sun rays feel hot. The smell of last night's rain has dissipated now.

"Ready?" Lila asks, sliding into the passenger seat.

"Ready?" Amelia glances at Bailey in the back seat ready to go.

He thumps his tail once, eyes alert on the road ahead.

"Good," Lila says, buckling in. "Because I have a feeling we're about to start hearing some echoes of the past."

Amelia starts the engine, her gaze fixes on the empty street as the diner fades behind them.

Somewhere out there, the truth is waiting, she has no intention of letting it remain buried.

6

The Safe-Deposit Key

The drive back to the Inn is quieter than usual. The last of the afternoon light glows through the windshield, painting the roadside trees in streaks of orange and red. Lila sits with her elbow propped against the window, chin in hand, while Bailey snores softly in the back seat. He's apparently satisfied with his afternoon of diner surveillance.

Amelia's thoughts replay Dottie's words like a scratched record. *Eric was always careful... too careful for that kind of mistake.* She could still picture the thin, incomplete file in Tom's hands, the empty spaces where reports should have been. It wasn't negligence. It felt deliberate.

When they pull into the Inn's gravel drive, the sun is beginning to dip behind the maples that line the property, scattering golden light across the yard.

"I'll just be a minute," Amelia says, turning off the engine. "I need to get something."

Bailey perks up, tail thumping expectantly.

"No, detective," she says with a smile. "You and Lila hold down the fort."

Lila gives an exaggerated salute from the passenger seat. "Copy that. If anyone suspicious walks by, Bailey and I will interrogate them through interpretive barking."

Amelia laughs and climbs out of the car. Inside, the Inn smells faintly of cinnamon and clean linen, comforting in a way that steadies her nerves. She walks to the kitchen, where the old box still rests on the corner of the counter, just where she left it after Edna's visit.

Carefully, she lifts the lid. Inside lay the hunter's certificate, range card, photograph, and that small brass key, number 312, stamped neatly on one side. Amelia turns it in her fingers, feeling its cool weight against her palm.

"Time to see what this unlocks," she murmurs to herself.

She slips the key into her pocket, then reaches for her phone and types a message to Edna:

Can you meet us at the bank? Bring Eric's birth and death certificates, might help us get into a box if it's in his name.

The reply is almost instant: *On my way. Fifteen minutes.*

When Amelia steps back outside, Lila has moved to the driver's seat and is idly flipping through a local events flyer she found in the glove box.

"Everything okay?" she asks.

"Better than okay," Amelia answers as she slides into the car. "We're heading to the bank. Looks like you're driving."

Lila perks up immediately. "Ooh, are we robbing it or just investigating?"

"Investigating," Amelia grinning as she fastens her seatbelt. "Let's hope we don't end up doing both."

The Maplewood Savings & Loan sets on the corner of Main and Cedar, a two-story brick building with gleaming brass handles and a clock that runs five minutes slow. It has been that way for as long as Amelia can remember.

Edna is already waiting near the entrance, clutching a manilla envelop to her chest. She looks steadier today—determined.

"Got your paperwork?" Amelia asks as they meet up on the steps.

Edna nods. "Birth certificate, death certificate, and my driver's license. I hope it's enough."

Inside, the bank is quiet, the air a bit cool and faintly scented of lemon polish. The woman behind the counter, a smiling brunette with glasses, greets them warmly.

"Morning, ladies. How may I help you today?"

Amelia steps forward. "We're hoping to check on a safe-deposit box, possibly in the name of Eric Hampton. This is his mother, Mrs. Hampton, she found this key in his things."

The teller's smile dims slightly, "That does look like one of our keys." She scans the documents Edna hands over. "Oh,

I am sorry for your loss, let me check," she explains and disappears into the back.

Lila leans over the counter to whisper, "I feel like we're in one of those spy movies. Should we have code names?"

"Absolutely not," Amelia says under her breath.

The teller returns a few minutes later, a ring of keys in her hand. "You're in luck. We do have a box registered to Eric Hampton. Since you have proof of relation and the death certificate, I can give you access to its contents."

She gestures toward a heavy metal door at the far end of the lobby. Amelia notices Lila's barely-contained excitement as they followed.

Inside the small private viewing room, the teller places the metal box on the table and leaves them alone.

Amelia exhales slowly. "Here we go."

Edna turns the key with shaking hands. The lock gives a soft click, and the lid lifts easily.

Inside, resting on a bed of brown paper, is a roll of cash—fifties and twenties bound with a rubber band and a small, folded piece of notebook paper, torn from a notebook.

Lila whistles softly. "Someone's rainy-day fund."

Amelia ignores her, picking up the paper and unfolds it. "It is just names or initials, nothing else."

HR, Marcus, Jimmy, Jonah, Virgil.

They exchange glances.

"HR," Amelia murmurs. "Hank Ross?"

Edna's hand trembles slightly. "Maybe one of these, is the man in that photo... the man with Hank and Eric."

Lila points at the next name. "Jimmy—that's got to be Jimmy Dale, the mechanic. Dottie mentioned him."

"Jonah?" Amelia asks.

Edna's eyes widen slightly. "Jonah Ritter, was the bank manager. He helped me close Eric's account after his death." She looks toward the lobby as if she could still see his desk through the years. "He never mentioned there was a safe-deposit box. I would've asked for it. And the last name on the list?" Edna asks. "Virgil?"

Lila frowns. "Probably Virgil Reed, the baker. He's got more frosting under his nails than secrets."

Amelia refolds the paper carefully and slips it into her pocket. "We'll leave the cash here for now. But the list, we need."

They exit the vault, and Edna returns the box. At the counter, Amelia asks quietly, "Is Jonah Ritter still with the bank?"

The teller shakes her head as she looks down. "No, I'm afraid Mr. Ritter passed away two years ago. Sudden heart attack. His wife still lives nearby, though—Marian Ritter, over on Sycamore Street. Lovely woman."

Edna thanks her softly, her expression a mixture of sadness and curiosity.

"Well," Lila starts off as soon as they step outside. "If the man's gone, maybe his widow knows what secrets he kept."

"Worth a try," Amelia agrees as they walk toward the car.

Marian Ritter's cottage is about three blocks away, half-hidden behind a tangle of rose bushes now stripped bare for winter. The small white house leans slightly to one side, its porch is crowded with potted plants, wind chimes, and a rusty birdcage without a bird.

Marian opens the door, a cautious inch, when they knock. Her pale blue eyes dart between them.

"Yes?"

"Mrs. Ritter?" Amelia asks gently. "I'm Amelia Hartford. This is Lila Benson, and Mrs. Edna Hampton. We're sorry to intrude, but we were hoping you might help us with something regarding your late husband's bank and Edna's late son."

Marian hesitates, then opens the door wider. "Come in, then. But I can't promise I'll be of any use."

Inside, the house smells faintly of lavender. The furniture is neat, though a fine layer of dust coats the shelves.

Edna explains quietly how her son had died in Maplewood and that Jonah had been the one to help her close his accounts. Marian listens with folded hands, her gaze distant.

"Jonah was a good man," she says finally. "But he carried secrets. I always suspected they had something to do with the bank, though he never said. He'd get phone calls late at night and take his ledger out to the shed. Wouldn't let me near it."

Amelia exchanges a glance with Lila. "The shed?"

Marian nods and points toward the kitchen window. "Out back. He kept it locked. Even after he passed, I couldn't bring myself to go through everything. Too many memories."

Before Amelia could respond, Bailey suddenly stands rigid, ears at attention and staring toward the back of the house. A low growl rumbles in his throat.

"Bailey?" Amelia asks, following his gaze.

A second later a faint creak of a door hinge. Marian's eyes widen. "The shed!"

She rushes toward the back door and flings it open. "Hey! What are you doing?"

A shadowy figure jerks upright near the shed and bolts for the trees. Bailey lunges forward, barking furiously. Amelia grabs his collar just in time to keep him from taking off after the intruder.

"Stop!" Marian shouts, her voice echoing through the yard. But the figure is already gone, into the line of trees behind the house.

Amelia's heart is hammering as she turns back toward Marian. "Do you keep anything valuable in there?"

"Only papers," Marian says, breathless. "Jonah's things." She pulls a ring of keys from a hook by the door and marches toward the shed. "Come on, it's time to look."

Amelia and Lila follow, Bailey strains against the leash, still pulling toward the trees.

The shed door has three separate locks. Marian's hands tremble a bit as she fits the keys, one after another, and finally pushes the door open. The air inside smells stale with hint of dust and oil. Stacks of banker's boxes line the walls, each neatly labeled in Jonah's tidy handwriting.

Marian moves toward a back corner and slaps her hand on a group of boxes marked simply with numbers. "These," she begins to explain softly. "He told me once that some things were better left unseen. I think these are the ones he meant."

Amelia crouches to read the writing—loan records, account ledgers, miscellaneous. Each box is heavy with the weight of paper and secrets.

"We shouldn't stay here," Lila suggests, glancing nervously toward the trees. "Whoever that was could come back."

Amelia nods. "She's right. Can we take these boxes with us to look through them?"

Marian hesitates, then give an approving nod. "Take what you need. Maybe it's time the truth came out."

They each carry a box back toward the cars. Edna cradles hers like something fragile, her expression distant but resolute.

"I'll go through these tonight at the motel," she offers. "I've got nothing but time and coffee."

Amelia smiles faintly in agreement. "Just please be careful. And lock your door."

As they walk, Bailey pauses suddenly, ears high. His gaze fixes on the edge of the yard where the trees thicken.

Amelia follows his stare, but sees only the faint shimmer of movement, a branch swaying, maybe, or a figure slipping out of sight.

A chill traces its way down her spine.

"Let's go," she says quietly.

They place the boxes in Edna's car. "We will talk tomorrow, I will let you know if I find anything in these records," Edna says as she waves to them and pulls out. They smile, nod and wave as she drives off.

Lila opens the car door and ushers Bailey inside. "That's twice today he's been on alert," she murmurs. "Either someone's following us, or that dog's developing a sixth sense."

Amelia starts the engine, eyes scanning the rearview mirror. The trees stand still now, silent and ordinary in the fading light.

"Maybe both," she replies softly. "But either way, we're being watched."

7

Unwelcome Attention

The sky over Maplewood has flattened into a pewter-gray lid by the time Amelia pulls into the gravel drive. The maple leaves that still cling to the trees rattle like paper coins, and Bailey give a happy huff the instant he recognizes home. Lila climbs out on the passenger side, and heads to her car. Amelia lets Bailey out and heads toward their door.

"I'll swing back later," Lila yells out, cinching her scarf against the chill. "If inspiration strikes, text me. If danger strikes, call me. If pie strikes—save me a slice."

Amelia manages a smile and a wave as she replies, "Go. I've got Bailey. He's braver than both of us."

Bailey wags his tail, as if to confirm, then trots up the steps toward the door, nose working the air.

"Text me when you're settled," Lila adds, then hops in her car and pulls away, taillights blinking once as she rounds the bend toward her place.

Inside, the Inn's warmth does its usual work. Amelia fills the copper kettle and puts it on the stove, lights a cinnamon candle in a jar by the window which produces a soft glow and pleasant scent. She tidies up a bit while waiting for the whistle. Bailey curls up on the rug by the hearth, knowing Amelia will be joining him in the parlor with her tea any moment.

The sun is setting, the moon already visible as she gazes out the window while steeping her fresh cup of tea, the familiar smell and warmth of the cup is relaxing and comforting. She makes herself comfy in her favorite parlor chair and pulls out her phone to text Lila. She is indeed settled in.

By dusk, the Inn has softened into evening rituals. Two couples return from the antique shop on Main, cheeks pink from the wind, and Amelia hops up and greets them in the foyer for some idle chatter.

"Yes, Sylvia's display case was beautiful, no, you probably shouldn't buy the cracked mercury-glass mirror unless you like your reflection in a funhouse," one guest explains to the other. Bailey leans companionably against their knees, receiving his due tribute of compliments. An older gentleman comes in from an early dinner at the steakhouse on Route 9 and reports, with solemn authority, that the apple crumble was "nearly as good as Dottie's." Amelia is suitably impressed.

“Well, it sounds like you all had an eventful day, I will be in the kitchen if you need anything,” Amelia announces as she heads in to fix herself some dinner.

She prepares something simple in the kitchen: tomato soup, buttered toast, an apple she slices thin and fans out beside her bowl. Bailey sits with all the patience of a monk until the last bite disappears; then he puts his head in her lap, and she scratches the warm place behind his ear that always makes him sigh.

“Tomorrow,” she tells him, as she walks to the cabinet for his dinner, “we go back to Tom with what we’ve got and see if he has found anything.”

Bailey’s tail thumps once against the cabinet. Then he rushes to his bowl which Amelia is filling for him.

The Inn quiets with the kind of hush Amelia loves—shower pipes sending brief, friendly clatters through the walls; a floorboard creaking as someone crosses to a dresser; the soft percussion of pages turning in the library. She does a last sweep of the common rooms, collects two stray mugs, and flips the sign on the front door to *Quiet Hours*. Outside, the driveway lays black and glossy from a short evening sprinkle, the gravel shining like peppered sugar under the porch light.

She is halfway to the staircase when Bailey freezes, ears forward, nose pointing straight at the door. In the near-silence, Amelia hears it too: a low engine idling. Holding steady. Close.

"Who is here now?" She crosses the foyer and lifts the edge of the curtain. A pickup sits just beyond the wash of the porch light—dark, older model, cab windows reflecting nothing but the house's own tired glow. Bailey's growl starts low, a warning rumble that vibrates through her hand where it rests on his shoulders.

The truck doesn't move. A full breath. Two. She doesn't recognize it.

Amelia unlatches the door and steps onto the porch, Bailey at her knee. The cold snaps her fully awake. "Hello?" she calls out, trying to sound like a woman who had neighbors, a phone, and a dog with very large teeth.

As if her voice trips a wire, the engine revs and the truck rolls away, smooth at first, then too fast, tires crunching and spitting gravel. It vanishes between the trees without so much as a brake light's apology.

Bailey's growl fades to a suspicious sniffing of the steps and railing. Amelia swallows. She waits a minute longer, counting to thirty twice, then locks the door and checks it twice for good measure.

"Someone's nervous," she tells Bailey. "As am I, a bit." She gives him a hug and they both climb up the stairs to her room.

Amelia changes for bed, while Bailey seems to be conducting a security sweep of the room, sniffing everything. Bailey stops and settles himself on his bed at the end of hers. She climbs into bed, tosses and turns a bit and then drifts off to sleep.

Morning brings the ordinary blessings: the warmth of the oven, the clink of plates, Lila's entrance. "I'm here, alive, caffeinated, and scarf on brand!" And, of course, the four-way choreography of a full breakfast: maple scones, herbed eggs, bacon, and fruit that pretends not to be out of season. Amelia is good at mornings. They give her something to do with her hands while her mind arranges itself around the bits and pieces of what she wants to do today.

Guests trickle down, eat happily, and trickle back out with their own plans: more antique hunting, a drive to the overlook, a lazy hour with library books beside the fire. Amelia carries their stories like pebbles in her pocket: small, smooth, grounding. Between refills, she types a quick message to Sheriff Granger.

How's it going? Could you stop by the Inn when you're free?

The reply comes fast: *Sure, mid-morning.*

She sets the phone down, finding herself experiencing a bit of relief. She plates a scone for Lila, who will inevitably arrive without breakfast. By nine-thirty, the dining room is empty. The house hums with a particular peace, that always makes Amelia think of her grandmother; quiet as a quilt, strong as the threads that hold it together.

A firm knock brings her to the front hall.

Mayor Tuttle standing on the porch in a charcoal overcoat, hat in hand, an expression that tries to pass for benevolent and lands somewhere near pained. Bailey, at Amelia's heel, sniffs him once and then sits, a neutral verdict.

"Miss Hartford," Tuttle says, removing his hat. "May I come in, for a moment?"

He doesn't wait for an answer. He steps into the foyer, his gaze sweeping the portraits on the wall, the polished banister, the bowl of apples she sat out on the entry table. He gives a similar vibe to a buyer at a house showing, not a neighbor at all.

"I hope this is a good time," he says, but in a tone which indicates no concern for the answer. "I wanted to touch base about... yesterday."

"Yesterday was a long day," Amelia replies. "Which part?"

He presses his lips together. "The, ah, meeting at Marian Ritter's house. I'm sure you're aware that people notice things. I only hope you're not planning to make a habit of... stirring the pot."

"Mrs. Ritter invited us into her home," Amelia says with an added roll of her eye. "We didn't break in."

"Of course," Tuttle responds quickly. "No one would suggest otherwise. I'm simply urging caution. Emotions are running high. Old wounds. The last thing Maplewood needs is another kerfuffle."

"Kerfuffle?" from a voice behind him. "I love a good kerfuffle."

Lila breezes in, scarf bright as a sunrise, cheeks pink from the cold. "Mornin', Mr. Mayor. Are we regulating the weather now, or just women's curiosity?"

Tuttle draws himself taller. "Miss Benson."

"Mayor," Lila chirps. "You're right on time. We were just about to..." She sniffs the air. "Eat scones. You like scones, don't you? Or are those against the bylaws?"

"I'll leave you ladies to your morning," Tuttle announces, the words losing life as he speaks them. "Please, Miss Hartford. Consider the town's peace."

He tips his hat and withdraws, the door closing on a breath of frosted air. Lila watches him through the sidelight glass until he reaches the sidewalk.

"I swear," she insists, "if that man could wrap Maplewood in plastic to keep it fresh, he would."

Amelia exhales. "He's worried. That's his job."

"And... your job is breakfast," Lila jokes, snagging the waiting scone as soon as she steps into the kitchen. "Which, thank goodness, you take more seriously."

Bailey lifts his head, ears high and now standing at attention. Then, a knock, but not at the door, it is coming from the side of the house.

Then, quick steps coming from the porch and stopping. Bailey rushes to the front door, Amelia and Lila in quick pursuit.

As they reach the door, Bailey barks, deep and furious. Amelia moves in front of him, "Back!" she yells to Bailey, hand low at his chest. She grabs the door knob, "I am going to take a look."

"Are you sure that is a good idea?" Lila cautions.

"Wait!" a voice behind them calls out. It is Mr. Kent. "I am going with you. You are not going out there alone, Bailey obviously senses something not normal."

Amelia nods and opens the door; she, Mr. Kent, and Bailey step out on the porch. "I don't see anything," Amelia announces after she looks around. But, Bailey heads out onto the porch, and then moves to the side of the porch where the sound emanated from.

"Seems like he knows where we need to look," Mr. Kent says as he follows Bailey.

When they come around the corner of the Inn, they see a large pile of wildflowers tied up with a black ribbon laying at the top of the porch steps. "What is this?" Amelia asks out loud as she kneels down for a closer look. Mr. Kent does the same.

Bailey has calmed, but is now off the porch sniffing around as they inspect the "gift" that lies before them.

"There's a note attached," Amelia notices as she picks up a small paper scroll tucked between the stems and the ribbon. She unrolls it, as Mr. Kent looks over her shoulder.

"**LET IT STAY BURIED**," Mr. Kent reads it aloud. "Well, wonder who else doesn't want you meddling in the past?"

"Good question, but they appear to be gone now," Amelia stands up. "We should go back inside and let everyone know its okay out here." Bailey is already on his way back to the porch, having found nothing in the yard.

Mr. Kent agrees and they all head back inside.

Lila is still at the door and the other guests have joined her, all waiting for their return. "Well, what is that? Did someone leave you flowers?"

"I think the message to back off was more the point than the flowers," Amelia replies.

"I agree," Mr. Kent admits. "It was to be expected that more than just the Mayor was going to be unhappy about your inquires."

"That means there is definitely something that needs to be dug up," Lila offers, "so we better get out the shovels."

"Yes, it appears this is confirmation that someone is hiding the truth," Amelia agrees.

Everyone follows Amelia back to the kitchen. "Let's get back to breakfast. Apologies for the interruption," Ameila says as she lays the flowers and note on the counter.

As the guests resume eating and sipping their coffee, the sound of footsteps catch their attention, heading to the front door.

Bailey just heads to the door, without any sign of concern.

"It must be someone we know. Bailey is in greeter mode, not pursuit," Lila reassures everyone.

As Amelia follows Bailey to the front door, it opens before she reaches it.

Sheriff Tom Granger fills the frame, winter coat unbuttoned, breath fogging faintly.

"Good morning. I am here as requested," Tom announces as he hangs his coat and hat on the wall rack.

"You should come on into the kitchen and see the package that was anonymously left for me a bit ago." Amelia signals him to come into the kitchen where everyone is whispering and eating in between their speculations.

Amelia points to the flowers on the counter, directing Tom's attention to them. He looks at them and then sees the note. "You," he says, pointing at Amelia, "attract more trouble than a pie contest."

"Good morning to you too," Lila remarks, now fully over the momentary tension. "Want a scone?"

Tom pinches the bridge of his nose, then accepts the offered scone, because even sheriffs require carbohydrates.

He uses a handkerchief to pick up the note and read it. "I am going to need to take this and the flowers back to the station..." He looks at Amelia, "... but I don't think we will get anything off this stuff. Looks like the flowers were picked from a field and nothing remarkable about the ribbon or note."

Tom's gaze softens as he looks toward Amelia. "You okay?"

"I'm fine," Amelia replies, as she simultaneously realizes it's true. "Mostly annoyed with the idea that some flowers are going to stop me from finding the truth."

"I can work with annoyed and glad it was a floral delivery and not something worse. Is this what you asked me to come over for?"

"Oh, no, that was before the flowers were delivered and before Mayor Tuttle dropped by to 'urge caution' and to 'keep the peace.'"

"Don't worry, we are heeding both recommendations," Lila chimes in making the guests chuckle quietly. "In fact, we are heading out for more shovels shortly."

Even Amelia chuckles before responding, "I'm glad you're here though," Amelia begins to explain. "I asked you over to talk about yesterday. Let's go to the parlor." She starts walking in that direction and Tom follows her.

"So, we visited the bank, with Edna, yesterday."

"What was at the bank?"

"Turns out, her son had a safe deposit box, Edna found the key in Eric's things," Amelia continues. "We accessed it with Edna's documents. Inside was a roll of cash... and a list. First names and initials: HR, Marcus, Jimmy, Jonah, Virgil."

Tom's jaw engages, a small click in front of a larger thought. "Hank Ross. I can't say I know a Marcus. Jimmy Dale. Jonah Ritter. Virgil Reed." He exhales through his nose. "That's a strange group of names."

"We left the cash," Amelia adds. "Only took the list."

"Good," Tom says. "I'll need a copy. And I want you to hear me clearly, Amelia." His voice lowered. While I understand that these flowers seem harmless enough, someone isn't just nervous—they're warning you off. I need you to let me handle the next steps."

"I know," she admits, and she did know it was coming. She also knows that knowing is not the same as obeying. "I won't do anything reckless."

Lila had moved into the doorway to the parlor to see how it was going, Lila coughs into her scone. "Define reckless."

Tom adopts a patience honed by exactly these two women. "I'll talk to Jimmy again. And I'll put out feelers on whoever Marcus is. In the meantime, I want the Inn doors locked and a deputy cruising past every hour."

"We're fine," Amelia gently assures. "But thank you."

He pauses, one heartbeat, two, as if there were a hundred unsaid words in the space between them, none of which belong to the active investigation. Then he nods once and steps back.

"At least, try to stay out of trouble," he reminds her.

"I know, I'll try," Amelia replies.

"You never try," he mutters, ever so quietly, as he shakes his head walking out the door. Then, down the steps, across the yard, back to the business of keeping order in a town that would rather have quiet than truth.

While Amelia and Tom were in the parlor, the guests managed to finish up and head out for their day's excursions.

Amelia and Lila are in the kitchen clearing the table and washing up, when someone knocks, precise, polite, and unexpected.

Lila freezes. “If that’s someone else telling us to back off, we really need to pick up our pace.”

Bailey’s ears perk up, but he doesn’t growl. Amelia glances at him, a read she trusts more and more, then crosses the foyer and opens the door. “Looks like Bailey is okay with the knock,” she calls back to Lila.

A young woman stands on the porch, wind-ruffled hair tucked into a wool cap, eyes wide but steady. She is holding a folded piece of paper in one hand.

“Ms. Hartford?” she asks. “I’m Josie Banks. I heard you were asking about Eric Hampton.”

Bailey’s tail gives a single, decisive thump, then he moves toward her, tail wagging.

Amelia steps back, heart settling into that curious hybrid of dread and relief that has become familiar in Maplewood, the feeling of a door to the past opening. “Come in, Josie. I’m just about to make some tea.”

8
Into the Woods

"I'm sorry to show up unannounced. Dottie at the diner said you were asking about Eric Hampton," explains Josie.

"That's true, dear. Would you like some tea?" Amelia offers as she signals for her to have a seat at the kitchen table.

Bailey greets Josie with a polite sniff, tail wagging once before resuming his spot beside Amelia's leg. Lila perches on a stool at the kitchen counter, watching with open curiosity.

"You knew Eric?" Amelia asks as she pours Josie a cup of tea.

Josie nods. "For about a year, maybe a little less. We met at the bakery. Virgil used to hire me to help out on Saturdays, and Eric was always stopping in for pastries. He said it made him look respectable." A small, sad smile flickers across her lips. "He was funny like that, charming one minute, brooding the next."

"Were you dating or just friends?" Lila chimes in.

"We were friends first, then we were starting to get more serious." She lowers her head, "I think it would have grown more, but, well as you know, then he was gone."

"I am sorry that happened. Did you come here to tell us something specific?" Amelia asks.

"Oh, not really, I just want to help if there is anything I can help with," Josie explains, as she wipes a tear from the corner of her eye.

"Did he ever talk about anyone named Marcus?" Amelia asks. "Or maybe Hank Ross?"

Josie hesitates for a moment. "Hank, yes. The Sheriff back then. He and Eric went hunting sometimes. Eric said Hank was helping him 'get on his feet.' I don't recall a Marcus." She pauses a moment, glancing at the list Amelia places on the table. Then she adds, "Virgil is the baker I worked for back then and Eric helped him with big deliveries from time to time, Jimmy was around a lot back then, he and Eric were friends."

Lila leans forward. "And Jonah?"

Josie frowns. "The banker? No. But Eric mentioned 'money problems' once. Said Hank and some others were making a side business of sorts. I didn't ask for details, I didn't want to know."

She set her tea cup down, hands trembling slightly. "But I can tell you where they spent most of their time, Hank's old hunting cabin, about five miles out past Brenton Road."

She reaches into her jacket and unfolds the paper she brought with her, a rough hand-drawn map with a looping road and a small square marked *Cabin*. "If you follow this road," she explains, pointing, "you'll see a rusted mailbox with a bullet hole through it. That's where you turn off. The cabin's maybe a quarter mile down the dirt path. Eric and I went there a few times."

Her voice softens. "It wasn't fancy. Just a place for drinking, talking. But he always seemed nervous there, like someone might show up."

Amelia's pulse quickens. "Would you be willing to tell the Sheriff this?"

Josie instantly shakes her head. "I can't. I already told too much back then, and it didn't help. But… if you go, maybe you'll find something. I really need to get back to town." She heads toward the door.

Amelia follows her with Bailey right behind.

She hesitates at the door, turns back to Amelia, "Be careful. That cabin brings bad luck."

"We will, thank you for coming by and helping," Amelia closes the door behind her and turns back to look at Lila.

Lila jumps off the stool, "Let's go! No sense in waiting. Grab your coat."

The road out of Maplewood winds past fallow fields and rows of bare trees, the last tatters of autumn hanging on like stubborn secrets. Amelia drives, following Josie's rough map while Lila scrolls through her phone in search of landmarks.

"You know," Lila begins, "for a town that prides itself on being quiet, we sure have a lot of bodies buried under nostalgia."

"Please don't say 'bodies.'"

Lila grins. "Fine. 'Misdemeanors of mortality,' then."

Bailey huffs from the back seat, head resting on the window ledge as though he, too, thinks the word choice questionable.

The rusted mailbox appears exactly where Josie said it would, a relic of some long ago abandoned route. Amelia slows and turns onto the narrow dirt lane. The tires crunch over fallen leaves and dried up weeds. Branches hang low, brushing the car roof with dry, whispering fingers.

"This is exactly how scary movies start," Lila mutters.

"Relax, we're not characters in a movie."

"Spoken like a woman in the first act," as Lila shakes her head.

The cabin appears at the end of the road, half hidden by overgrown brush, its roof sagging slightly, and one shutter hangs askew. Amelia pulls the car over off the path. They look at each other and then the cabin.

"Ready?" Amelia asks.

"As I will ever be, let's do this."

Bailey's paws on the door window, he is ready too.

The front steps creak beneath their weight. Amelia eases the door open.

Inside, the air smells of dust and stale tobacco. Light slants through broken blinds, striping the room in pale gold. Empty bottles litter the floor near an overturned card table. Two folding chairs sit against the wall beside a shotgun mounted on a rack above the fireplace.

Lila peers around, her face crunches up as she takes in her surroundings. "Charming. Really sells the hunter's paradise vibe."

Amelia's eyes stop and linger on the shotgun. It seems off, she just isn't sure why. She steps closer to get a better look, there is something on the stock. She can't quite make out if it is a branding or a hand engraving, but it's not a plain smooth gun stock. She takes out her phone and snaps a quick photo. She wasn't sure why, only that she wants to look at it again, later.

"Bailey, stay close," she calls out, as he begins sniffing along the baseboards.

"Look at this," Lila says, gesturing to the small pile of matchbooks scattered on the floor near the hearth. Each one bears the same logo, *Rusty Anchor Bar, Brenton, KS.*

"That's two towns over," Amelia replies, "not exactly a short drive for a beer."

"Unless they were meeting someone there," Lila offers. "Or picking something up. Didn't Eric do odd jobs, including deliveries?"

Bailey gives a sharp bark and trots to the door, nose high.

"Uh-oh," Lila says. "The nose knows, something."

They follow him outside, stepping over a half-collapsed porch rail. Bailey continuously sniffing the ground, he leads them through a patch of weeds toward a stand of trees about five hundred feet behind the cabin. He sniffs around in a circle, then begins digging furiously at a spot near the roots of a fallen tree.

"Hold on, boy," Amelia says, then she crouches down beside him. Her stomach gurgles a bit as her fingers feel something smooth, damp, firm, not fleshy but plastic. She sighs and the tension in her shoulders lets go. She clears away enough dirt to reveal a thick black trash bag, tied tight at the top.

Lila's eyes wide open. "Please tell me it's not a head."

Amelia gives her a look, shaking her head. "This isn't *that* kind of story." She pulls the knot loose. Inside were several rolls of cash, crisp bills despite the dampness of the soil, and a handful of small baggies filled with white tablets.

"Money and pills," Amelia murmured. "Not exactly necessary for hunting trips."

Lila stares. "So Eric was mixed up in something illegal. That might explain the shady circumstances surrounding his 'accident.'"

Bailey suddenly barks sharp, with a warning, "Woof, woof, woof." His ears flatten, body tenses.

"Someone's here," Amelia whispers.

From somewhere near the cabin comes the screech of tires. They sprint back through the trees in time to see a what appears to be a truck, dark blue, older looking, as it skids onto the dirt road and roar away, dust flying out from behind it.

"Was that the same truck from last night?" Lila gasps.

"I don't know," Amelia answers. "But whoever it was might have been watching us."

She reaches her car and freezes, her hands fly onto her head. Bailey runs up to the car, sniffing and whining. Two tires flat, the rubber slashed clean through.

"Well, that's convenient," Lila adds as her shoulders and head drop and she signs heavy.

Amelia checks her phone. "Great! No signal."

"Of course not. We're in the middle of nowhere. Do you have the emergency flare or should we start a smoke signal?"

Amelia rolls her eyes but a smile forms without her consent. "Come on. The main road's only a mile or so. We can walk until we get service."

She tucks the bag into the trunk, hiding it beneath a blanket, and they head off down the road with Bailey leading the way.

As they walk, the conversation circles back to the discovery.

"Maybe Eric was running drugs," Lila offers. "Or skimming money from whomever he worked for. Maybe Hank found out and..."

"Or he was in over his head and wanted out of whatever it was," Amelia interrupts. "That's what the letter suggested."

Lila glances over. "You really think Hank was part of it?"

"I think he knew more than he ever put in that file."

The wind rustles the trees overhead. Bailey's steady footfalls sound louder in the hush of the woods. Silence falls over them, neither knowing what to say or speculate. Amelia is running the situation over in her head, wondering if the person who slashed the tires already knew what was hidden or did they lead this person to something they were trying to find? Surely this money had been buried for some time, perhaps prior to Eric's death, but what if it hadn't, what if they just walked into the middle of something else?

The distant growl of an engine reaches them, snapping her out of her thoughts. Amelia turns, relief washing over her as Sheriff Tom Granger's SUV comes into view. He slows and stops beside them, leaning out the window.

"Let me guess," he says. "Car broke down, no cell service, and a curious streak a mile wide?"

"Something like that," Amelia replies, trying not to smile.

"Hop in. Josie stopped by the station. Told me about that map. Figured I'd better check on you before you managed to get into trouble."

Bailey jumps into the back seat as though he'd been expecting the rescue all along.

On the short drive back toward the cabin, Amelia fills him in, the bag Bailey unearthed, the cash, the pills, the tires, and the truck speeding away.

Tom's forehead crunches. "You didn't touch the pills, did you?"

“Of course not,” Amelia replies. “We just… peeked.”

Lila nods. “Very professionally. Minimal peeking.”

Tom parks beside Amelia’s disabled car and gets out. He pulls out a pair of gloves from his jacket pocket. “All right, let’s see what you found.”

Amelia opens the trunk and hands him the bag. He loosens the knot, looks inside, and exhales softly. “Well, that’s not aspirin.”

He ties the bag again, eyes narrowing at the trees. “This changes things. I’ll log it as evidence and send it to the lab.”

He steps back to the SUV and grabs the radio. “Dispatch, it’s Granger. I need a tow out on Brenton Road, near mile marker twelve. Two flat tires, vandalism. I am bringing two women back with me to give statements.”

As he talks on the radio, Amelia and Lila begin clearing out her car—umbrella, a tote of books, a spare jacket, all the things she can’t stand to leave behind.

Tom hangs up and turns to them. “Tow’s on the way. I’ll give you a ride back to the Inn. Which, if I recall, is where you are supposed to be, keeping your head down today.”

“Thanks,” Amelia says, as she recalls the conversation from earlier.

He nods but his usual easy smile is absent. “You two got lucky today. Whoever was out here didn’t want you finding that bag.”

“That’s what worries me,” Amelia mumbles under her breath.

Tom looks at her in the eyes, something unreadable, uncertain. "It worries me too."

"All right, everyone back in, we are stopping by the station so you can both fill out a report," Tom instructs as he is getting into the driver's seat.

The ride back to town is quiet, except for Bailey's soft panting and the rhythmic click of the turn signal.

The stop at the station is brief and uneventful. As they ride back to the Inn, Amelia is troubled, her mind will not calm. While she is worried about who is following them, watching them, she also realizes she let her curiosity get the best of her. It could have been worse and Tom did ask her to lay low and be safe. But on the other hand, they did find something, something that may help move the needle on Eric's case.

When they reach the Inn, Tom idles by the porch.

"I'll make sure your car gets to the shop," he says. "Call me when you hear from them about the tires. And stay close to home tonight, all right?"

Amelia nods. "We will."

Lila gives him a cheery wave. "Thanks for rescuing us from certain doom, Sheriff."

Tom's expression softens a little. "You're welcome. Though next time, maybe call me *before* heading into the woods."

"We'll try," Amelia replies, though they both knew how that usually went.

As the SUV pulls away, she stood for a moment beside Bailey, watching the taillights fade into the distance. The cold air biting at her cheeks, but her thoughts burning.

The bag of money and pills. The slashed tires. The file that never told the full story.

She sensed Tom's growing concern. That told Amelia more than words ever could.

The "accident" story is cracking, one truth at a time.

9

Rumors and Revelations

Inside Maple Leaf Inn feels like a sanctuary again. Bailey's tail drums against her leg while Lila leans against the kitchen counter. Amelia is replaying the morning with the disbelief of someone who'd just walked out of a crime scene and into a cookbook.

"Well," Lila speaks finally, "I don't know about you, but I've reached my weekly quota of 'near-death-by-flat-tire.' Should we start again tomorrow with coffee and fewer felonies?"

Amelia laughs softly. "I wish I could leave it at that, but we still have a list of names and too many questions."

"I guess that means a bakery stop," Lila says. "Virgil first, Sylvia after. And since your car's at the shop, I'll chauffeur. Think of it as my turn to drive the getaway car."

Bailey perks up at the word *car*. Lila winks at him. "And you, little detective, get a window seat."

They tidy up, then head into town. Maplewood's main street glimmers with the faint gold light of late afternoon. The air carries a crisp promise of winter and the familiar comfort of chimney smoke curling skyward. Amelia rolls down the window an inch, letting Bailey's nose work the wind as they pass familiar storefronts.

"Virgil first," Lila says, turning the corner. "He's our sugar-coated alibi for being nosy."

The bakery bell jingles as they step inside, trailing the scent of cinnamon and maple syrup. Virgil Reed looks up from behind the counter, flour dusted on his apron like snow. His smile reaches all the way to his eyes.

"Well, if it isn't my two favorite detectives," he says with a smile. "And Officer Bailey."

Bailey's tail wags as if on cue.

"Afternoon, Virgil," Amelia greets him warmly. "We wanted to ask you about Eric Hampton. You remember him, right?"

Virgil's expression shifts, his smile fades to a look of nostalgia or maybe regret mingling. "Oh, Eric, yes, I remember. He and that Josie girl used to come here about every week. Always sat by the window, shared a cinnamon roll and two coffees, argued over who got the bigger half."

Lila grins. "Sounds romantic."

"It was," Virgil adds, his tone deepens as his gaze lowers. "Until it wasn't. They stopped coming together after a while. Eric started showing up alone, looking... well, troubled. Hands shaking a bit sometimes. Didn't talk much."

Amelia's face mimics his concern. "Did he ever do any work for you?"

"Sure did," wiping his hands on his apron. "Helped me with deliveries. Big church orders, school fundraisers, you name it. He was reliable too, until one day he wasn't. Just disappeared.

"Did you ever see him with anyone besides Josie?" Amelia asks.

Virgil thinks for a moment. "Jimmy Dale sometimes. Nice enough boy, but jittery. They were friends, I believe. You might ask Sylvia down the block at the antique shop. Eric used to make deliveries for her too."

"Thanks, Virgil," Amelia smiles. "You've been a big help."

"Of course," his gaze moves to Bailey. "And for the record, my door's always open for investigators with paws."

Bailey accepts a biscuit with the dignity of a man handed a medal.

Lila waves back at Virgil as they leave the bakery.

Sylvia Donnelly's antique shop is only three doors down, the kind of place where time seems to hang in the air between ticking clocks and the faint scent of lemon polish. The bell over the door jingles, announcing their arrival.

"Ah," Sylvia says, appearing from behind a shelf of porcelain teacups, her dark hair swept into its usual elegant twist.

"If it isn't Maplewood's resident detectives, and the most well-behaved dog in town."

"Flattery will get you everywhere," Lila chimes in, brushing a bit of dust from a nearby display.

"We're just following a thread," Amelia explains. "Virgil mentioned you knew Eric Hampton."

Sylvia's expression darkens slightly. "I did. He and Jimmy Dale helped move that cabinet there, the one with the etched roses." She taps a manicured finger on the glass. "But, afterward, a few small pieces went missing. I suspected them both, but I could never prove anything. I reported it and I kept my eye on them after that."

"Hank Ross ever follow up on your report?" Amelia asks.

Sylvia lets out a short laugh, the sound brittle as crystal. "Follow up? He told me to keep my shop locked and my mouth shut. Said thefts were common this time of year, as if criminals worked on a holiday schedule." Her gaze softens. "I always wondered what became of Eric. Shame he didn't live long enough to grow out of his youthful mistakes."

Lila's tone, gentle but probing, as she asks, "You ever notice anyone else around back then? Maybe hanging around with them?"

Sylvia hesitates, tapping a ring against the glass case. "There was a man I didn't recognize. Big fella, scar by his eye. He stopped in once, asking after Eric. I told him Eric didn't work for me anymore. He smiled, but it didn't reach his eyes. I remember I locked the door after he left, he gave off a vibe that made me uneasy, that is the only time I remember seeing him."

Amelia and Lila exchange a quick glance. The scar. The same one Amelia had gotten a glimpse of, on the man outside the diner.

"Thank you, Sylvia," Amelia says as she reaches out and touches her arm. "You've helped more than you know."

"Be careful," Sylvia urges. "Whatever you're stirring up has been quiet for a long time; it might want to stay that way."

Lila responds as they are heading out the door, "We'll be careful, but it is about time for some noise around here."

"Let's grab dinner," Amelia points to the diner.

"Perfect." Lila signals Bailey to follow.

The bell over the diner door chimes them into warmth and chatter. Dottie turns to see who is coming in, as she drops off an order at the cook's window. She waves her towel like a greeting flag, while flashing her normal bright smile.

"Well, if it isn't the Maplewood Posse," she says. "You hungry or investigating?"

"Both," Lila answers, sliding into a booth. "Mostly hungry."

Bailey finds a spot under the table, where Dottie promptly appears with his usual treat and a wink. "Detective's orders?" she asks, handing Amelia a menu. "Soup's hot, pie's fresh, and coffee's strong enough to make you confess your sins."

"Perfect," Amelia replies. "We'll take two soups and keep the coffee coming."

Lila perks up and adds, "Don't forget we want some pie, too!"

As they wait for their food, they trade notes from the day, their find in the woods, Virgil's memories, Sylvia's warnings, the scarred man, her slashed tires. A pattern was forming, slowly but surely, like pieces of a puzzle, not quite fitting in place, yet.

Lila leans back against the booth. "So, Eric was working for Virgil, maybe doing errands for Sylvia, close with Jimmy, and probably mixed up with old Hank. That's four out of five names from the list."

Amelia nods, stirring her coffee absently. "And every one of them has a reason to keep quiet. Hank, especially. Whatever was happening back then, he was in the middle of it."

Bailey gave a low huff, as if agreeing.

"Then we keep following the trail," Lila says. "But first? Food."

Across town, Sheriff Granger rubs a hand over his face and looks at the file laying open on his desk. The words were the same as yesterday, but they felt different now. Incomplete. Wrong.

He hears the office door creak open and stands up, as Edna Hampton steps inside, holding her purse close. "Deputy Ruiz said you wanted to see me," she says softly.

"Please," Tom motions her to the chair across from his desk. "Thank you for coming in."

Edna's composure holds, but her eyes are weary. "Has something happened?"

Tom hesitates, then opens a small evidence bag on the desk. Inside was the copy of the photo from Eric's box and a separate bag containing the list from the safe deposit box Amelia had copied. "Mrs. Hampton," he begins gently, "yesterday, Ms. Hartford and Ms. Benson visited a cabin your son used to frequent. Their dog uncovered a buried bag containing a substantial amount of cash and narcotics. I am not certain if this all ties together with the past or if something current is going on but, I'm reopening your son's case."

Edna blinks, color drains from her face. "Narcotics? Are you saying Eric was..."

"I don't know," Tom responds quickly. "That's what I want to find out. There's money in his name, connections to multiple townspeople, and missing reports from the original file. The only way to make sense of it is to start over."

She nods slowly, her fingers tightening around her purse strap. "He wasn't a bad boy," she whispers. "He made mistakes, yes, but... he wasn't bad."

"I believe you," Tom assures her. "But there's more here than one man's mistakes. And I need your help. Do you still have any papers, notes, or letters from his things?"

Edna nods. "At the motel. Records from the bank. I've been reading through them. I can bring them in."

"That would help a lot. The more we can piece together, the sooner we'll know who's responsible—and what really happened."

She exhales with relief. "I never thought I'd hear someone say that. Ten years of silence, and now..."

"Now we do it right," his voice quiet but firm. "This time, nothing gets swept aside."

He rises, offering her a small smile and his hand. "Mrs. Hampton. I'll be in touch later, I will send a deputy over to pick up the bank records, if you think of anything else, reach out."

"Thank you, Sheriff," she said softly, standing and shaking his hand. "For listening and questioning."

Edna leaves. Tom stares at the open file for a long moment before reaching for the phone. He dials a familiar number and waits.

"Hank Ross," the voice on the other end announces, gruff and irritated. "This better be good."

"It's Sheriff Granger," he says with authority. "I need you to come into the station. Now."

"What for?"

"Eric Hampton's case, I'm reopening it."

Silence on the other end. Then, "You've got to be kidding."

"I'm not," Tom replies. "We'll talk when you get here."

He hangs up before Hank can argue.

10
The Case Reopened

Back at Dottie's, the bell over the door jingles again. Amelia looks up from her coffee just in time to see Edna step inside, her purse clutched tight but her shoulders lifted just a little higher than before.

Dottie spots her and calls out, "Well, look who's back. Sit anywhere you like, hon."

Edna catches Amelia's eye and smiles faintly, crossing the diner to their booth. Bailey thumps his tail against the floor in greeting.

Lila slides over to make room. "Perfect timing," she says, "we were just about to order pie."

Edna manages a soft laugh. "Then I must be in the right place."

Amelia meets her gaze gently. "You seem different, better almost."

Edna nods. "The sheriff reopened Eric's case. He thinks there's more to find."

For a moment, silence from all of them. The noise of the diner, the soft clink of plates, the low hum of conversation, fill the air like an old song rediscovered.

Finally, Amelia reaches for her cup and lifts it in a quiet toast. "Then here's to finding it."

Edna smiles and sighs. "To finding it."

Bailey gives a soft, approving woof, sealing the promise between them.

Dottie arrives with fresh coffee all around, plus a saucer of whipped cream "for the officer." Bailey tries to be dignified about it and fails, earning a fond eye-roll from Lila.

"Tom asked us to bring in anything that might be relevant," Edna explains, folding and unfolding her napkin. "He's having a Deputy pick up the bank records from me." Pride and worry cross her face in quick succession. "He sounded... determined."

"That's Tom," Amelia says. "Quiet, but steady."

"And stubborn," Lila adds, "which for once is a compliment."

Across town, Tom Granger's stubbornness is on full display. He stands in the doorway of Interview Room B, arms folded, watching Hank Ross tip his chair back with a slouch that reads as either comfort or defiance. Maybe both.

"Ten years," Hank says, voice gravelly. "You bring me in to talk about a hunting accident from ten years ago? Don't you have potholes to ticket?"

Tom ignores the bait. "We're reviewing the case due to new information."

"What information?"

"That's the funny thing about an investigation," Tom says with a serious tone and expression to match. "We ask the questions."

Hank sits forward. "Go ahead, son."

Tom doesn't bristle at *son*. He simply lays a photocopy of the thin, original report on the table and, beside it, a clear sleeve with a scrawled list of names. HR. Marcus. Jimmy. Jonah. Virgil.

"You wrote this summary," Tom says. "No coroner's report. No ballistics. No chain of custody for the gun. Why?"

Hank's shrug is slow. "Because it was clear as day. Man shoots himself by accident in the woods. End of story."

"Funny, the truth usually uses more than half a page." He lets it sit, lets Hank feel the smallness of the old file. "We found cash and pills buried near a cabin you own. There's a safe-deposit box in the victim's name with more cash. The boy was tied to you and people you hunted with, he was using your cabin. Funny again."

Hank's eyes harden. "You don't like me, Granger, that's not a crime."

"I don't like incomplete work," Tom clarifies, voice even and firm. "That's what I'm fixing." He closes the file without looking down. "Don't leave town."

Hank snorts. "Where would I go?"

Tom doesn't answer. He opens the door and lets the silence follow Hank out of the room like a shadow.

Back at the diner, the shadow arrives ten minutes later.

The bell over the door gives a tired little jangle as Hank Ross steps in, hat pulled low, jaw set. Conversation dips, slightly, the way a pond stills after a rock drops into it. Hank scans the room, takes in the booth by the window, and his gaze snags on Amelia, Lila, Edna and the dog whose brown eyes don't blink.

Lila leans toward Amelia, whispers, "It's Hank."

"I know," Amelia murmurs.

Bailey doesn't growl. He watches, quiet and intent, as if memorizing the shape of the man, waiting for any wrong move.

Hank pretends not to notice them and orders a coffee to go, slapping cash on the counter like he is punishing it. Dottie doesn't pretend anything; she pours the coffee without a word and slides it across. Hank takes the cup and leaves in a gust of cold air as quickly as he arrived.

"No going back now," Lila announces, voice bright enough to hide a hint of nerves.

Edna unclenches her hands and reaches into her purse. "I brought something for you to see, before I take it to the Sheriff." She lays out photocopies she'd made at the motel's tiny business center: bank pages grid-lined with deposits and transfers. "There's a lot of money going in and out of accounts that list only an initial and last name. I matched them to my notes. H. Ross. J. Dale. E. Hampton. J. Ritter. The dates overlap."

Amelia leans closer. "Sources? Notes?"

"That's the problem," Edna says. "Deposits are cash. Transfers bounce between those accounts. No memos. No checks. Just numbers moving around to confuse anyone glancing at them."

"Classic shell game," Lila mutters. "Move it fast and act like it belongs."

Edna exhales. "I'll take my notes to Tom. They will be picking up the ledgers too. Maybe they can see what I can't."

"We should decide what to hand over from the box you brought with you," Amelia says gently. "The photo, the letter, the range card, they're personal. The key led us to bank evidence, so Tom already knows about that. But we haven't proved the rest is evidence yet."

Edna considers, then nods slowly. "You're right. He asked for anything relevant. I'll start with the bank boxes and the key to retrieve the cash from the safe-deposit box. If he needs the rest, he can ask."

"Good," Amelia agrees. "One step at a time."

Outside, the autumn light had slanted toward dusk, turning the storefront glass into sheets of gold. Dottie swings by with their pie, she had not forgotten.

"Fuel," she says, setting down plates. "You can't fight city hall, or our former sheriff, on empty stomachs."

They eat with the reverence pie deserves. By the time forks lie down, afternoon has melted into evening. Edna gathers her papers.

"I better get back to the motel," she says, determination steadying her voice. "The deputy will be by to pick up the boxes."

"We'll walk you to your car," Amelia says.

They stand as a group. Even Bailey seems to understand the ceremonial weight of it, the handing-of-torches moment where rumors become records and records become evidence.

At the curb, Edna squeezes Amelia's hands. "Thank you."

"We're not done," as Amelia returns the squeeze and her eyes fill with compassion.

"I know." Edna's smile thins with gratitude. "That's why I can breathe."

She drives off toward the motel, taillights like little red promises in the hazy dusk.

Lila checks her phone. "I should head home and draft while I'm actually inspired." She points at Amelia. "Call me when the car shop says your carriage is ready. I'm coming for the grand unveiling."

Amelia laughs. "It's two new tires, not a coronation."

"In this town, same difference," Lila plants a quick kiss on Bailey's head. "You keep her safe, Detective." Then she is off, scarf bright and blowing like a flag as she disappears down Main.

Amelia calls the auto shop. "Hi, I am checking on the Honda you towed in from Brenton Road?"

"Two new tires, mounted and balanced," the cheerful reply, barely audible over the compressor hissing in the background. "Keys at the desk ready for pick up."

"I'm on my way," Amelia says. She pockets her phone and looks at Bailey. "It's a short walk, let's go, boy."

Bailey answers with a wag so hard his tags chime.

They head down Maplewood's gentle slope toward the repair shop, two blocks after Main Street, a left, and a right to the squat cinderblock building with a hand-painted sign and a row of cars like patient steel cows. The daylight has thinned to slate, and the security light over the back lot blinks itself awake with a buzz.

They are rounding the corner when the bushes along the side chain-link fence rustle hard. Bailey's body transforms from loose to stiff; he plants his paws, ears rise and he stares. A shadow jerks up from behind the tangle, broad-shouldered, hooded, then bolts.

Amelia's heart takes a beat, once, hard. "Hey!" she calls, purely on instinct, while holding Bailey back.

A truck engine on the dirt lane behind the garage starts up and roars away, tail-lights flicking like a dare through the trees.

She exhales and crouches to smooth Bailey's ruff. "I saw him, too."

Inside, the shop smells of warm rubber and oil. A teen in a grease-speckled ballcap looks up from the register and grins like they were old friends.

"Ms. Hartford? Tires are on. We checked alignment, too. Road rage out there? Sorry about your flats."

"Thanks," Amelia says with a grin. "Is Jimmy around?"

The kid shakes his head. "Left a few minutes ago. Said he had to run an errand."

Amelia troubled by the echo of the fleeing figure like a tap on the shoulder. "Did he say where he was heading?"

"Nah." The kid slides a clipboard across the counter. "Sign here, please."

She signs, pays, and pockets the receipt, almost in a trance. As she leads Bailey to the car, she struggles to keep her mind from projecting suspicion onto every shadow. Jimmy could have been the runner. Or it could have been the scarred man again. It could have been Hank. It could have been someone she didn't know to fear yet.

Outside, the air is turning colder, sweet with woodsmoke. Amelia opens the door, Bailey hops in. As she drives the short way home, she relaxes a bit, absurdly grateful for the mundane click of her own turn signal.

At the Inn, evening's soft rituals about to begin. Porch light on. The faint thoughtfulness of a lamp in the front parlor. Bailey heads for his bowls; Amelia serves him his dinner. She puts the kettle on and heads upstairs. She changes for warmth, into a thick sweater and wool socks, then returns to the kitchen where the kettle is starting to sing. She pours the hot water into a mug, drops a chamomile bag to steep. She grabs a blanket and heads to the porch. Bailey follows and then settles at her feet like a hearth rug that breathes.

Beyond the pool of porch light, the trees are an arrangement of shapes varying in size. She looks into them with the feeling that the dark is listening back.

"This is too much," she says aloud, her words fog the air in front of her. Her grandmother's voice arrives not as memory but as a presence: *If you're able to help someone in need, then that is what you do.* "All right, Grandma," Amelia whispers, the words settling her heartbeat into pleasant rhythm. "I'll keep going." Her mind flips through the questions like pages. The shotgun at the cabin, why does it bother her? Why was it there, who did it belon to? Why had she known, without knowing, to take a picture? Who had been trailing them: the scarred man, Jimmy, Hank, or someone else entirely? And who sneaked up and left the warning? Was it a warning from a concerned person or a smokescreen from another?

Cars turn into the drive, bringing her guests back to their small comforts—library books, baths, the easy forgiveness of a warm bed. Amelia rises to greet them at the door, her blanket sliding from her shoulders like a shred of hesitation.

"How was the overlook?" she asks a couple with wind-reddened cheeks.

"Cold and perfect," they answer together, laughing.

"The kettles still warm, if you need some tea or cocoa to warm you up," Amelia offers, and the woman's entire posture softens with gratitude. She accepts some compliments on the scones at breakfast, answers one question about the best time to visit the antique fair, as if that were the most pressing mystery in town.

When the last guest has climbed the stairs, Bailey nudges her hip with the softness he saves for the end of long days. She turns off the porch light, locks the door, and stands a second in the friendly dark of the foyer, listening to the house remember how to sleep.

"Bed," she tells Bailey.

He leads the way, tail swishing like a metronome set to *peaceful.* Upstairs, Amelia pauses by the window and looks out over the dark yard toward the line of trees. They look like paper cutouts against the sky.

"Tomorrow," she whispers to herself, to the trees, to the town, to the thread of truth drawing her forward. "We keep going."

Bailey circles once at the foot of the bed and sighs himself into dreams. A heartbeat after, Amelia's eyes fall closed, too, her last thought a snapshot of a shotgun on a rack and a promise not yet fulfilled.

11

The Past Comes Knocking

The scent of cinnamon rolls and percolating coffee drift through the kitchen signals that the Inn is awake and ready for the day. Morning light spills through the windows, catching on the polished oak counters. Amelia runs her hand across the surface, remembering how her grandmother had refinished by hand decades before. Bailey snores under the table, one paw twitching in a dream, while Amelia ladles batter onto the griddle.

Her guests trickle in, faces fresh with sleep and the kind of cheer that only small-town mornings can conjure.

"Morning, Ms. Hartford," calls Mr. Kent, the retired history teacher who had declared the Maple Leaf Inn his favorite weekend escape. "Heard some interesting talk at Dottie's last night. Something about an old case being reopened?"

Amelia smiles, flipping a pancake. "Maplewood does love a good story."

"So, it's true?" asks Mrs. Kent, eyes bright. "You're helping the Sheriff?"

"I'm helping a new friend," Amelia replies carefully. "Just a friend trying to find some peace."

"Peace," Mr. Kent repeats knowingly, "is a rare thing once you start asking questions."

Amelia chuckles politely and brings out the orange juice. "That's why I stick to coffee. Questions require caffeine."

Bailey yawns, stretches, and wanders toward the door as it opens.

Lila breezes in, scarf trailing behind her like a comet's tail. "Did someone say caffeine? Or was that divine intuition?" She drops a kiss on Bailey's head and grins at the guests. "Don't mind me, just making sure Amelia hasn't solved another crime spree before breakfast."

The laughter from the amused guests loosens the air. Amelia rolls her eyes affectionately.

"Honestly, Lila," she says, "you make me sound like I keep a magnifying glass in my apron."

Lila plops onto a stool. "If the magnifying glass fits..."

The guests laugh again, and just like that, the morning is into its easy rhythm: coffee pouring, bacon crispy, Bailey stationed loyally beside his food bowl, watching the floor, as the self-appointed crumb collector.

By nine-thirty, two guests have checked out, luggage loaded into the back of a sedan headed toward Wichita. The others are heading off for the antique fair, waving as they exit. The Inn quiets, leaving behind an array of mugs, glasses, flatware and plates waiting for cleaning and the faint creak of the floorboards as they are gathered up.

Amelia is stacking dishes when a sharp, heavy knock rattles the front door. Not the hesitant kind of guests who've forgotten their keys, this was a sound that demands to be answered.

Bailey's head snaps up. He barks once, deep, warning and hurries himself, stopping between Amelia and the door, fur along his spine bristling.

"Easy," she tries to settle him, drying her hands. "Stay, boy."

When she opens the door, the cold morning air brings with it the unmistakable silhouette of Hank Ross. He stands on the porch, hat in hand, his expression carved from stone.

"Ms. Hartford," he says. "Morning."

Amelia's smile was polite, if not warm. "Good Morning, Sheriff Ross."

He adjusts his hat. "Used to be."

Bailey gives a low growl.

Amelia grabs his collar. "Can I help you?"

"Thought I'd stop by," his voice smooth but tight. "I had a chat down at the station yesterday. Then, seems your name is coming up more than I like around town, I can only assume you had a hand in pushing Sheriff Granger into this."

Amelia's stomach tightens, though she keeps her tone calm and firm. "Then, you'll also know I'm just trying to help Mrs. Hampton understand what happened to her son. I have nothing to do with what the Sheriff investigates, but I did hear he reopened Eric's case."

Hank's eyes, small beneath his brows. "Some things don't need understanding. They need leaving alone."

Lila appears in the hallway, still holding her half empty cup of coffee. "Oh, now this feels like the part in a movie where someone says, 'this town ain't big enough...'"

Hank's jaw twitches. "Morning, Miss Benson."

"Morning," Lila says sweetly. She pulls out her phone and, under the pretense of checking messages, thumbs the record button.

"Mr. Ross," Amelia says invitingly as she moves aside slightly. "Would you like to come in? I don't imagine this is the kind of conversation to have on a porch in the cold."

He hesitates, then steps inside, boots heavy on the hardwood. Bailey follows close, a silent sentinel.

"Coffee?" Amelia asks out of habit.

"No, thank you." He takes off his coat but doesn't sit. "I came to offer some advice. Stop digging into graves, Ms. Hartford. That's how good people get hurt."

"Good people," as she tilts her head downward and then looks upward at him, "usually don't have to worry about what's buried."

His mouth tightens before he replies. “You think you’re clever. Asking questions about old cases, nosing through evidence that’s not yours.”

“I think I’m thorough,” Amelia counters. “You wrote the only report on Eric Hampton’s death. Half a page, no coroner’s notes, no forensics. You didn’t even keep the gun. Why?”

His eyes flash, for a second. “Because it was a simple accident. A man trips in the woods, gun goes off. End of story.”

“No record of who collected the weapon, as I doubt it was left lying in the woods,” Amelia presses. “Or who identified the body. No mention of anyone else present. Were you there?”

“I was Sheriff then,” Hank said sharply. “I was everywhere, I knew the boy.”

“That’s not an answer.”

He steps closer, Bailey responds with a deep growl. Hank freezes, nostrils flaring, then smiles a tight cold stretch of lips. “You’ve got nerve, I’ll give you that. But you’ve got no right to question my integrity or my methods. I’ve kept this town clean longer than you’ve been alive.”

Lila speaks up from the doorway, voice mild. “You sure did. So clean you swept a few things right under the rug, didn’t you?”

Hank’s gaze snaps toward her. “Careful, Miss Benson.”

“Always am,” she says, deliberately smiling at him.

He turns back to Amelia. "You don't know what you're stirring up. Folks around here respect me. They'll see you as a meddler before they see me as a villain."

"I'm not interested in titles," Amelia exerts sharply. "Just truth."

"Truth," he repeats partially under his breath, as he puts his hat back on. "Truth's a funny thing. Changes depending on who's telling it." He puts on his coat as he heads toward the door.

He pauses, hand on the knob, looking straight ahead, "You've had your warning, Ms. Hartford. I suggest you take it."

He pulls the door shut behind him with a finality that echoes through the foyer. Bailey barks once at the sound, then sits down hard, tail flicking with agitation.

Lila waits until the footsteps recede from the porch. As she hits stop on the recording, she says exhaling, "Well, that was friendly. Should I file that under *veiled threat* or *villain monologue*?"

Amelia chuckles. "Somewhere between both, I think."

She turns toward the counter where the matchbooks from the Brenton Bar still lay in a neat little pile beside her notes. Hank's words clinging to her like smoke, but her eyes lingering on those matchbooks, another clue that refuses to fade.

"Looks like we keep digging," she announces.

Bailey thumps his tail once, solid agreement.

Lila grins. "You know, that's the villain's version of a confession we just heard, he is guilty of something, we just need to figure out how guilty."

Amelia nods in agreement, her smile returns, small but sure. "And I plan to prove it." She pauses. "Let's go find that bar, 'Brenton Bar.' I googled it and it's only about an hour and a half away."

"Yes, I'm in," Lila smiles and grabs her coat and another cinnamon roll from breakfast. "It's for the road," she explains.

Amelia chuckles and agrees, "Better grab me one too."

12
Banking on Secrets

The morning air stirs, a restless feel of late autumn, the kind that hints at frost without quite committing. Amelia carries a travel mug of coffee out to the car while Bailey bounces in hopeful circles at her feet, tail drumming on the porch rail.

"Relax, Sherlock," she tells him, opening the back door. "It's a fact-finding mission, not an adventure."

Bailey hops in anyway, ready for either.

Lila appears a moment later, scarf flying like a banner in the wind. "I brought snacks," she announces. "The kind that make car rides civilized."

"Coffee counts," Amelia adds.

"Not in my world." Lila holds up a paper bag that smells of Dottie's best scones. "Fuel, gossip, and pastry-based logic. That's how real detectives operate."

Amelia smiles despite herself, locking the Inn door behind them. "If we find any leads before noon, I'll credit the pastries."

Bailey gives a happy bark of agreement as they climb into the car, where he has been patiently waiting.

The highway out of Maplewood stretches under a pale November sun. Rows of stripped cornfields now golden wave in the breeze as they pass. The two women talk quietly, about the cabin, the list of names, and what they still don't know.

Lila tears a scone in half and hands it to Amelia. "We've got bankers, bakers, and possibly one candlestick maker," she jokes. "You think Eric's mother was right? That he really wanted out?"

"I think he was scared. With the letter and the hidden money, it all seems like someone planning an escape, not a scheme."

"Except escaping from whom?" Lila ponders.

Neither answer. The question rides with them all the way down the county road.

Meanwhile, in town, Marian Ritter stands just inside the Sheriff's office, clutching a worn shoebox like it might fall apart if she breathes wrong. She looks smaller than usual, her coat hangs loose, her gloved hands trembling slightly.

"Mrs. Ritter," Deputy Ruiz greets her, stepping from behind the counter. "Good morning. What can I do for you?"

"I… I found this," she begins to explain, setting the box on the desk. "Jonah's personal ledger, I think. It was tucked inside an old pair of his shoes, of all places." Her voice falters. "He must've wanted to hide it. The handwriting's his, no doubt about that."

Sheriff Granger emerges from his office at the sound. "Morning, Marian." His voice gentle, coaxing, "May I?" as he extends a hand.

She nods, removing the lid. Inside lay a narrow, bound notebook, its pages filled with tidy columns of numbers and initials. Some entries were underlined in red ink—others circled faintly, like reminders to be erased.

Tom turns a few pages, noticing he is becoming agitated as he reads. "These initials—H.R. and J.D.—they match Hank Ross and Jimmy Dale?"

"I think so," Marian replies. "Jonah always said bookkeeping tells stories, but sometimes they're the kind that shouldn't be told. I didn't want to believe he'd been part of anything wrong, but… he must've been."

Ruiz steps closer. "You did the right thing, ma'am."

Marian nods while looking down and now with the absence of the box to hold, clenches her hands together. "There's more, Sheriff. I've been getting strange calls lately, no one there when I answer. Someone breathing, or silence. And that man who tried to break into my shed the day the ladies came by… I can't stop thinking about it. Did the papers I gave them help you?"

Tom's brows scrunch together. "I haven't heard about any attempted break-in."

Marian blinked. "Oh. I assumed they told you. A man was trying to get into Jonah's shed while we were talking. He ran off when I yelled out to him from the house."

Tom's jaw tightens. "No, Mrs. Ritter. They didn't. And you didn't until now."

Ruiz looks up sharply. "You think it's related?"

"Could be," Tom says. He turns to Marian. "Did you get a look at him?"

"Only his back, he was tall. Dark jacket. Fast."

Tom nods, his mind ticking through possibilities. "All right. We'll look into it. And I'll keep this ledger secure. Thank you for bringing it in."

Marian smiles faintly, and relief softens her lined face. "I hope it helps."

"I'm sure it will." He walks her toward the door, "We'll let you know what we find."

Marian steps outside.

The Sheriff and Ruiz sit across from each other, the ledger open between them. The sunlight through the window catches on the faint red underlines across several pages.

"Coded accounts?" Ruiz asks. "Same pattern Edna Hampton found in her son's records, amid all the papers they collected from Mrs. Ritter's, cash deposits, small transfers, no descriptions."

Tom agrees. "Looks like payoffs or laundering. And the dates line up with Eric's time here in Maplewood."

He rubs his chin. "I've already requested the legitimate banking records for Ross, Dale, and Eric Hampton. If the same transaction amounts show up in both, we'll have proof of connection. But I'm betting the trail won't be that neat. I am betting this is an entirely different set of books—off the books."

"Never is," Ruiz admits. "What about the shotgun? I've gone through every inventory log from the old evidence storage, there is no record of a shotgun in evidence or ever having been logged in."

Tom's frown deepens. "So, the weapon that killed Eric was never booked, never tested, and never returned through proper channels."

"Which means someone made it disappear?" asks Ruiz. "Have you ever seen a case like this?"

Tom sits back, the chair creaks under his weight. "No, I have not. We're building a picture of a cover-up. Money moving through or around the bank. Missing gun. Threats to people with information or looking for answers."

Ruiz nods slowly. "And we've got one very unhappy former sheriff out there."

Tom's mouth thins. "Unhappy's not the word I'd use."

He stands, running a hand through his hair. "I'll call Amelia, get her version of what happened at Marian's, maybe she remembers something else."

He dials, waits, frowns. “Straight to voicemail.”

He tries again. Nothing.

“Can’t reach her,” he mutters.

“Want me to check her place?” Ruiz offers.

“Not yet. She’s probably out chasing another clue. I’ll try Edna first, she might know where they are.”

He dials Edna’s number.

Edna answers on the third ring, her voice faint but steady. “Sheriff?”

“Mrs. Hampton, I want to let you know the records you’ve been going through are already helping. Marian Ritter brought in one of Jonah’s ledgers, and I think it ties directly to your son and the others involved.”

“Oh, thank goodness,” Edna breathes. “There is still another box here that wasn’t picked up, do you want me to bring it over.”

“Actually,” if it’s all right, I’d rather swing by and collect it myself. That way we can secure all the originals as evidence.”

“Of course,” she says. “I’m at the motel.”

“Good. And…” he hesitates, lowering his voice, “have you noticed anything strange lately? Anyone hanging around or watching you?”

Edna thinks first. “Well, a truck passed by the motel twice last night. Same one both times, I think. Loud engine. But I didn’t get the plate.”

“Keep your door locked,” Tom instructs. “I’ll be there in the next fifteen minutes.”

"Will do."

The Maplewood Motel looks weary under the noon sun, paint peeling, curtains drawn. Edna meets him outside Room 3, holding the box of banking records and a safe-deposit key labeled with a simple 312.

"Here," Edna says as she hands it to him. "This was Eric's. You'll want to retrieve the cash from the bank, in this box."

"I'll log it as evidence," Tom said. "And we'll see what we can learn from these transactions. Maybe with this ledger we just received, we might have enough to follow the money trail."

"That's all I've ever wanted, for someone to follow up."

Tom gives a small nod. "You've done the right thing, pushing for answers."

He tucks the key into his breast pocket, shakes her hand gently, and starts back toward his SUV.

Halfway across the lot, the low growl of an engine makes him turn. A dark pickup comes around the corner fast, too fast, spraying gravel as it fishtails onto the main road. Tom catches a flash of the plate before it vanishes into the sunlight: **PE2...** and the rest too blurred to make out.

He stands still until the sound fades, the grit settling around his boots.

Out on the road, Amelia's car still traveling down the county roads, Bailey's head poking out the window as the fields rush by. Lila hums to the radio and unwraps another scone.

"Something tells me," Lila starts, "our Sheriff is having a day."

Amelia smiles faintly, watching the horizon. "Aren't we all?"

Bailey huffs in agreement, his tail flicking against the seat.

For a moment, everything appears ordinary, the kind of quiet between storms that makes Maplewood both beautiful and deceptive. But Amelia can't shake the sense that the circle around them is closing, quietly, efficiently.

Somewhere behind them, a truck's distant engine echoes through the hills.

13

A Friend in Trouble

Amelia's car is nearing the edge of town on the way to Brenton.

"Jimmy's garage is up ahead, isn't it?" Lila asks.

Amelia nods. "Might as well stop. Maybe he'll finally tell us what he's not saying."

"Or he'll bolt," Lila offers. "Either way, we'll learn something."

They turn into the gravel lot. The small auto shop looks the same as ever, half a dozen cars in varying stages of repair, an old Coke machine by the door, and the smell of motor oil baked into the air. Jimmy Dale stands near an open hood, wiping his hands on a rag, and freezes the moment he sees them.

Bailey gives a low growl as Amelia parks and they get out. His fur bristles slightly, more warning than aggression.

"Easy, boy," as Amelia opens the back door and grabs his leash.

"Afternoon, Jimmy," Lila calls out brightly, as if this were a casual social call.

He hesitates before managing a smile. "Ms. Hartford. Lila. Didn't expect to see you here."

"We were in the area," Amelia explains. "Thought we'd check in. Mind if we talk for a minute?"

Jimmy looks over his shoulder, then back at them. "Long as you don't mind grease."

"Comes with the territory," Amelia says.

She follows him to the workbench, Bailey staying right against her leg, then in front of her once she reaches Jimmy. Lila stays within earshot but close enough to intervene if needed. The air inside smells of gasoline, rust, and nerves.

"I wanted to ask you about Eric Hampton," Amelia begins. "And about Hank Ross. And a man named Marcus."

Jimmy stiffens. "Marcus? Haven't heard that name in a long time."

"But you *have* heard it? Do you know his last name?

"Sorry, I don't, he isn't from around here."

Disappointed, she redirects, "You and Eric were friends, weren't you?"

He nods slowly. "Yeah. Met him when he first moved here. He was a good guy, made some bad choices, but who doesn't?"

"Do those choices include working with Hank or Marcus?"

Jimmy's hands tighten on the rag. "Look, folks talk. But Eric got mixed up in something nasty. Real nasty. I told him to walk away, but he wouldn't. Said he had a plan to make it right." His eyes glance to the bay door as if expecting someone to be listening. "Then one day he's dead. That's all I know."

"Do you think his death was an accident?" Amelia asks.

Jimmy looks at the floor. "I think he got in over his head. And I think some of the people he trusted weren't who they said they were. That's why I keep my head down now."

"Scared?" Lila jumps in.

He laughs without humor. "Lady, I been scared for ten years."

Lila leans against a post, studying him. "You know, we are heading to Brenton next. There's a bar there, the Rusty Anchor. Eric's name came up around it."

Jimmy's reaction is immediate. His face goes pale, and his hand clenches around the rag until the fabric twisted. "Don't," he says sharply. "Don't go there. That's not a friendly place. It's dangerous. People mind their own business because they like living. You start asking about old names, you might not drive back out."

Bailey works his way between Jimmy and Amelia, his tail lowers.

Amelia exchanges a look with Lila. "We'll stay clear," she says smoothly.

Jimmy relaxes only a fraction. "Good. Leave it alone. Please."

Lila chimes in, "We promise, no need to have a heart attack over it."

Amelia offers him a small smile, slipping a card from her pocket. "If you think of anything that might help, call me. Anytime."

He stares at the card like it might bite him. "I'll... think about it, I really don't know more than what I have said." He doesn't look at them, just keeps looking down at the card in his hand.

Jimmy suddenly looks up, "Oh there is one thing you might look into here in town. Eric had his share of trouble, but he wasn't a bad guy. Just got mixed up with the wrong crowd. He and Hank had multiple confrontations back then, maybe there's something there?"

"Thank you, sounds like a good place to look," Amelia responds.

"You better remember, how small towns work. Everybody's got secrets. Best not to dig too deep," Jimmy advises.

Lila chimes in, "We will be careful, besides the Sheriff is on the case now, too."

"Thank you for talking with us, you have been very helpful," Amelia says as she and Lila turn and head for the car.

Jimmy nods and waves as they head back outside.

As they climb back into the car, Lila lets out a low whistle. "Well, that was uncomfortable."

Amelia nods. "And revealing."

Bailey settles into the back seat, but his ears were still high, as if he'd absorbed the tension too.

Before they pull out, Amelia's phone chimes, a text from Tom. *You neglected to tell me about the man and the shed. What else are you not telling me?*

Amelia winces. "It's Tom, he's not thrilled. He found out about the incident at the shed."

Lila leans closer. "You going to tell him about the matchbooks? The bar?"

"No," as she types a reply. *You're right, I should have mentioned it. I'm sorry. I'll fill you in later. Promise.*

She hits send and tosses the phone onto the console.

Lila arches a brow. "So, we're not going?"

"No, I just said we're not. Which means we absolutely ARE. But we'll take the long way, so if anyone's watching, they think we're heading somewhere else."

Lila grins. "Sneaky. I approve."

"Remind me to hate myself later," Amelia mutters, turning back toward the highway.

The road unfurls ahead, the fields giving way to denser trees and the occasional billboard promising *cold beer, warm food, good times.*

"Jimmy looked a bit terrified," Lila says. "Like someone's watching him."

"Maybe someone is," Amelia admits. "I think he may know more than he is saying. That 'plan to make it right'? That's key. No way Eric doesn't tell his best friend exactly what his plan is."

"More troubling is why he is so against us going to this bar," Amelia ponders out loud.

"I thought that was telling too." Lila murmurs. "I think you're right; he knows more."

The road to Brenton winds past a patchwork of open fields and thin woods, the landscape still gloved in the gold and brown of late fall. The sun sits high but faint, a pale coin behind drifting clouds. Amelia grips the wheel lightly, her eyes flicking through the road signs as Bailey's head pokes out the rear window, ears flapping like mismatched sails.

They drive in thoughtful silence for several miles before Lila reaches for the radio. "Too much thinking. Music therapy time."

Country twang fills the car, Bailey's content to sigh in the background. The hum of the tires and the rhythm of the songs softened the edge of their thoughts until the sign appears ahead:

RUSTY ANCHOR BAR – COLD BEER & LIVE MUSIC – OPEN 11AM–MIDNIGHT

The parking lot is half-empty, a scattering of pickup trucks and motorcycles lined up against the curb. The bar itself is a squat brick building, its paint peeling but its neon sign still buzzing like a tired heartbeat.

"Charming," as Lila rolls her eyes.

A smaller sign near the door reads *No Dogs Allowed.*

"Well, that's discrimination," Lila proclaims. "Come on, Bailey, we'll stretch our legs. Text me if you see any brawls or mysterious men."

"Will do," Amelia says, sliding out of the car.

Inside, the bar is dim but clean. The faint smell of beer and fried onions linger in the air, mixed with the ghost of old cigarette smoke. A jukebox glows in the corner, its music low and lazy.

A waitress approaches, wiping her hands on a towel. "You new around here?"

"Passing through," Amelia answers. "Actually, I'm looking for someone who might've been a regular a while back. Eric Hampton?"

The waitress frowns, thinking. "Don't know the name. But I've only been here about a year." She jerks her head toward the far wall. "If he's been here, he's probably on that wall. Go take a look, regulars' photos, from way back."

The wall is covered in overlapping snapshots, Polaroids, and prints—hundreds of faces frozen mid-laugh, mid-toast, mid-life. Amelia's gaze travels across the collage until a flash of familiarity stops her cold.

She sees him. Eric Hampton. Smiling, arm slung around Hank Ross, the former sheriff. Eric looks just like he does in the picture Edna brought with her. Between them stood a burly man with a scar near his left eye. All three dressed in hunting gear, grinning like they'd won something.

Amelia leans closer, studying the photo. The image is actually identical to the one in Edna's box, only this one has a jagged corner missing, as though someone had tried to tear it off the wall.

A few pictures down, another photo catches her eye: Eric again, this time beside Jimmy Dale, both kneeling beside a deer, grinning. Looks like the same day, same clothes, same hats, only Jimmy is in this one. She realizes Jimmy must have been the one taking the photo that Edna has.

Her pulse quickens. Jimmy must know who this mystery man is, he'd been *there*, hunting with them, maybe this is the Marcus he mentioned.

Amelia takes a quick photo of both pictures with her phone, then scans the rest of the wall. Jimmy appears together repeatedly with this man, different times, different seasons. Once at a poker table. Once outside the bar, holding bottles. Always together. Jimmy knows this man, well. She wonders what is their connection. So is that why Jimmy told them to stay away or is there another reason?

"Find what you were looking for?" the waitress asks, walking up beside her.

"Maybe, Do you know any of these guys?" She points to the photos of Jimmy and the mystery man.

The waitress peers closer. "Those two? Yeah, they still come in. Once a month, maybe. Always sit at the end of the bar. Don't talk much."

“I know this one, but do you know who this is,” as she points to the unknown man in the photo with Jimmy.

“Only his first name, it’s Marcus.”

Amelia’s stomach tightens. “If they come in again, could you call me? I’m helping someone look into an old case.” She hands the woman a card with her name and number. “If you remember anything, even small details, I’d really appreciate it.”

“Sure thing. But you be careful, honey. Those two don’t seem like friendly company.”

“I will,” Amelia said.

Outside, Lila and Bailey are waiting near the car. “That was quick,” Lila points out. “Find anything?”

“Oh, just a whole wall of ghosts and a big fat lie,” Amelia states with a scowl on her face.

They get back into the car, and Amelia tells her about the photos; Jimmy, Eric, Hank and the mystery man, identified as Marcus, all intertwined across years.

“So, Jimmy *was* there the day that photo was taken,” Lila realizes. "He was the one behind the camera.”

“Exactly, and it proves he’s lying about who and how much he knows.”

Lila almost jumps up in cheer. “That’s big. Think Tom will see it that way?”

“Eventually, but first, I need to put the pieces together. We can’t accuse anyone until we know what we’re holding.”

They drive the long road back to Maplewood in silence, the sky deepening into dusk as they approach town. The lights of Main Street come into view; Bailey yawns loudly, signaling his disapproval of long mysteries without snack breaks.

"I hear you," Amelia says. "Home stretch, then dinner."

About fifteen minutes later, the porch light glows soft and welcoming, as they pull into the Inn. Lila stretches her arms above her head. "I'm heading home before I turn into a pumpkin. You sure you're okay?"

"I'm fine," Amelia assures her, though her mind is far from calm.

Lila takes off waving as she pulls out. Amelia and Bailey head inside.

She puts on the kettle, pours Bailey's food into his bowl, and gets out a mug for herself and leaves it with a tea bag by the stove. While Bailey enjoys his dinner, she heads to the office to print the photos from her phone.

The kettle sings as she finishes up. She pours the steaming water over the bag in her mug to steep. "Let's go, boy." She heads to the parlor, settles into her favorite chair. Bailey stops in front of her, for his fur fluffing and rubbing and then curls up at her feet.

The Inn is quiet, save for the distant creak of old wood and the low hum of the heater. She spreads the photos across the coffee table, studying them one by one.

Eric. Jimmy. Marcus. Hank. Four men tied together by one day at least on the one day, but likely more.

Her gaze drifts to the photo from Edna's box. Jimmy wasn't in it because he'd taken it.

Guests peek in to say good night, their footsteps padding upstairs, laughter muffled by the walls. When the last door shuts, the Inn seems to sigh itself to sleep.

Amelia sits a moment longer, Bailey's head on her foot, the flicker of the fire painting the room in gold with moving shadows.

Her phone buzzes. Unknown number.

She answers. "Hello?"

Jimmy's voice is tight, breathless. "Meet me at the diner tomorrow at noon. Don't tell Hank, or anyone."

"Jimmy—wait—"

But the call dropped.

Bailey lifts his head, ears forward.

Amelia sets her phone down slowly. "Well," she whispers, "tomorrow's about to get interesting."

14

The Diner Stakeout

The smell of blueberry muffins and maple-glazed bacon floats through the Inn's kitchen, wrapping itself around the soft hum of morning conversation. Amelia moves easily between the stove and the long farmhouse table, her rhythm steady. The coffee poured, fruit arranged, muffins cooling in neat rows. Bailey keeps close at her heels, pausing only to sniff the air approvingly.

Amelia shelters herself in the normalcy of her morning routine, an escape from all that fills her mind.

"Morning, Ms. Hartford!" calls out one of her weekend guests, a retired teacher with a fondness for crossword puzzles and gossip. "Saw Sheriff Granger's car parked down the street late last night. Another mystery afoot?"

Amelia smiles, keeping her tone light. "I'm sure he was just checking on the neighborhood. It's nice to have the sheriff nearby."

From under the table, Bailey gives a low *woof* as if confirming her diplomacy.

Before she can answer another question, the front door bangs open and Lila sweeps in like a gust of wind wrapped in a floral scarf and energy. "Do not panic," she declares, "but I think we're about to have a very interesting lunch."

Amelia turns, wooden spoon in hand. "Good morning to you, too."

"Morning? Hardly. I've been up for hours, thinking about your late-night phone call."

Amelia's eyebrows rose. "Which one?"

"The one that ended with 'Don't tell Hank.' That one!" Lila's tone hovers somewhere between excitement and scandalizing curiosity. "You said Jimmy called you out of nowhere, said to meet him at the diner at noon, then hung up. That practically *is* a mystery novel title."

Several guests glance up from their plates, interest visibly piqued.

Amelia sighs, lowering her voice. "*Lila, not so loud.*"

"What? They love this stuff!" Lila whispers, but loudly enough that the nearest couple pretend to butter their toast while leaning closer. "It's just a little stakeout, right?"

Amelia shoots her a look, but it was too late.

"Stakeout?" echoes Mrs. Kent, eyes wide open, bright with intrigue.

"Oh, heavens," Lila says sweetly. "Just a figure of speech. We're not actually spying on anyone. Well... not much."

Mr. Kent lowers his newspaper. "If you're investigating another case, I think we deserve priority seating for the next mystery book club meeting."

Lila moves toward him conspiratorially. "I'll put you on the waiting list."

Amelia presses a hand to her temple, fighting a smile. "Breakfast first, gossip second. Bailey, keep an eye on everyone."

Bailey wags his tail once, solemnly accepting the assignment.

By the time the guests finish their coffee and head out for their day trips, the kitchen has returned to quiet. Amelia wipes her hands on a towel and turns to Lila. "All right, spill. What exactly do you think Jimmy wants?"

Lila perches on a stool, legs crossed, scarf trailing down her back like a story waiting to be told. "Confession. Blackmail. A proposal. Take your pick."

Amelia arches a brow. "You think Jimmy Dale is proposing to me?"

Lila shrugs. "You'd be surprised what people do under pressure. But seriously, he sounded desperate, right? My bet is he's ready to talk. Or warn us. Probably both."

Amelia exhales slowly. "That's what worries me."

Lila claps her hands once. "Then we go in prepared. I'll bring my notebook. You bring your calm 'I run an inn but can also interrogate murder suspects' smile.'"

Bailey barks softly, tail thumping.

"And Bailey," Lila adds, "brings the intimidation factor and his impeccable sense of timing."

Amelia shakes her head, but a smile tugs at her lips. "All right. Let's go before you decide we need disguises."

"Too late," Lila says, snatching her sunglasses off the counter. "I already brought props."

The diner is in its late-morning lull, coffee cups half-full, the air humming with the soft sound of silverware and conversation. The scent of grilled onions linger from the breakfast rush. Dottie wipes down the counter, humming along to the oldies station, and looks up when Amelia and Lila walk in.

"Well, look who's back," she announces, her grin bright. "You two should get frequent-diner cards. Coffee's already brewing."

"Thanks, Dottie," Amelia says, sliding into a booth with Bailey curling at her feet. "We're waiting on someone."

"Oh, a secret rendezvous!" Dottie teases. "Should I dim the lights?"

Lila chimes in, over the table. "Make that *double-strength* coffee, Dottie. We might be here a while."

Dottie laughs and leaves them with two steaming mugs. The warmth seeps into Amelia's hands, steadying her. Noon is only fifteen minutes away. Every time the bell over the door jingles, she looks up, half expecting Jimmy's anxious face to appear.

"You think he'll show?" Lila asks, stirring sugar into her coffee.

"He said noon," Amelia replies. "That's not a lot of time to change your mind."

"Fear does funny things," Lila murmurs.

The bell jingles again. Amelia's head lifts... it is Tom. He walks in, eyes scanning the room, uniform crisp and expression unreadable. When he sees them, a flicker of exasperation crosses his face.

"Of course," he says, as he approaches their booth. "I should've guessed."

"Good morning, Sheriff," Lila says with a bright smile. "You're just in time for our stakeout."

Tom sighs, sliding into the booth opposite them. "I don't even want to know what that means."

"Jimmy called me last night," Amelia offers up. "He wanted to meet here at noon. He said not to tell Hank."

Tom's brow furrows. "And you're telling me this *now*?"

"I was going to text you, but I didn't want to scare him off. If he's finally ready to talk."

Tom holds up a hand. "I get it. Just... next time, loop me in before lunch, all right?"

Bailey whines softly under the table, as if seconding the request.

Tom gives him a small pat on the head. "At least one of you listens."

Dottie comes by with the coffeepot. "Sheriff," she says, filling his mug. "Nice to see you. Everything all right?"

"Just following up on some business," he replies in a calm tone. "Nothing to worry about."

"Mm-hmm," she is clearly unconvinced but intrigued. "Well, if this business comes with pie, holler."

She moves on, the three of them sit watching the door. The minutes slip by. Twelve-ten. Twelve-twenty. Twelve-thirty.

Lila drums her nails against the table. "Maybe he chickened out."

Tom frowns, pulling his phone from his pocket. "I'll call the station. Ruiz said he'd send someone to swing by Jimmy's shop today."

But before he could dial, Dottie returns, worry flickering behind her usual cheer. "Sheriff," she whispers. "You might want to hear this. Word came in from the gas station on Maplewood Road, Jimmy's garage got broken into last night."

Amelia's stomach drops. "Is he all right?"

"Don't know yet," Dottie says. "But there's glass everywhere and no one's seen him this morning."

Tom stands immediately, already fishing his keys from his pocket. "Stay here. I'll check it out."

"Hold on," Lila shouts, standing too. "We can help."

Tom gives her a look that could curdle cream. "You can *stay here.*"

Amelia rises beside her. "Tom, wait... he called me for a reason. If he's scared, he might reach out again."

"I'll let you know what we find," he says firmly. "Just... don't go looking for him on your own. Promise me that much."

Amelia hesitates. "All right. Promise."

As he hurries out, the diner atmosphere seems to contract from the noise of his departure. The door bangs shut, the rumble of his engine fading into the distance.

Lila slumps back into the booth. "Well, I hate that we're right."

Amelia stirs her coffee, watching the swirl fade into stillness. "He knew something. Something important."

Bailey rests his chin on her knee, eyes soft and loving.

Dottie appears again, setting a plate of pie between them without asking. "Eat, it's what folks do when the world doesn't make sense."

Lila manages a small smile. "Wise words, Dottie. I'll add them to my memoir."

By the time they finish the pie, the diner has filled with chatter again, people ordering lunch, laughter bubbling near the counter. The world, relentless in its normalcy, moves on.

But for Amelia, every sound in the diner is distant. She looks toward the window, the empty street beyond, and recalls Jimmy's voice on the phone, tight, urgent, terrified, "*Meet me at the diner tomorrow at noon.*"

She made it. And he didn't.

15
A Trail Gone Cold

The first chill of late afternoon drifts through Maplewood by the time Amelia and Lila reach Jimmy's garage. The place is cordoned off with yellow tape, its front window shattered into a glittering scatter of glass. Two patrol cars sit parked out front, lights pulsing softly like distant heartbeats.

Tom stands near the open bay door, coat collar turned up, face set in a grim line. Deputy Ruiz is beside him, scribbling notes into a small pad.

Amelia's heart drops at the sight of the broken window. "Tom?" she calls softly.

He turns. The tension in his shoulders eases a fraction. "I thought I told you to stay at the diner."

"You did," she admits, "but staying put has never been our strong suit."

Lila gives a small, apologetic wave. "We brought moral support," she adds. "And Bailey."

Bailey wags his tail once, then sniffs the air, his expression changing from happy-go-lucky to alert.

Tom sighs but doesn't send them away. "We've been here half an hour. Jimmy's truck is gone, tools scattered, office door was forced open. Looks like he left in a hurry or someone made sure he did."

"Was anyone hurt?" Amelia asks.

"No sign of blood," Ruiz jumps in. "But the neighbors heard yelling around midnight. By the time anyone looked, the lights were off."

"Yelling?" Lila repeats. "Did they recognize a voice?"

Ruiz shakes his head. "Said it sounded like two men, maybe three. Hard to tell."

Bailey pulls gently at his leash, nose low, tail stiff. Amelia follows his movement with her eyes. "He's onto something."

Tom crouches beside the dog. "You got a scent, buddy?"

Bailey's ears perk up, then he moves toward the edge of the lot where a patch of gravel meets the thin strip of woods behind the building. Barely visible beneath the leaves, lay a torn scrap of fabric, dark blue, grease-stained, familiar.

"Jimmy's coveralls," Ruiz shouts, lifting it carefully into an evidence bag.

Amelia's pulse quickens. "So, he was here when it happened."

Tom straightens. "Yeah. But not when it ended."

He looks past the trees toward the faint trail that disappears into the woods. "If he ran, maybe he left us a direction."

Lila frowns. "Or maybe someone took him that way."

Either way, they don't have long to wait. Within an hour, a search team gathers, half a dozen deputies, a couple of volunteer firefighters, and a few townsfolk who heard the news and refused to stay home. Amelia and Lila join the group, flashlights in hand, Bailey out front like he was born for the job.

The woods are quiet but uneasy, the kind of quiet that feels borrowed. Leaves crackle underfoot, and the cold seemed to settle deeper as they move forward.

"Over here!" someone calls out, a voice sharp.

They follow the sound until they reach a clearing about a mile in. There, caught on a branch, is another shred of blue cloth, and beside it, a wrench half-buried in the dirt.

Ruiz bends down and picks it up. "Could be from the shop."

Tom takes it, turning it in the light. "Could also be a weapon."

Amelia's chest tightens. "Tom, what if Jimmy tried to defend himself?"

He meets her gaze. "Then we'll find out."

The group spreads out, combing the undergrowth for any other signs. Bailey leads Amelia and Lila along a narrow path that winds toward the old hunting cabin, his nose working the ground and the air furiously.

Lila shivers, pulling her jacket tighter. "We're really doing this again, aren't we? Back to the woods, following the dog, like moths to a very bad flame."

Amelia smiles faintly. "Maybe this time we'll find light instead of fire."

But when the cabin comes into view, the air smells faintly of smoke.

Bailey barks, pulling forward.

"Hold up," Tom calls from behind them, hurrying over.

Amelia points toward the thin plume curling from the cabin's chimney. "Someone's been here recently, using the fireplace."

They approach cautiously. The door hangs ajar, its hinges blackened. Inside, the air is thick with the acrid scent of burned paper. Ash coats the hearth, the remains of what looks like an opened small metal box charred by the fire.

Lila covers her nose. "I'm guessing that wasn't for roasting marshmallows."

Tom uses the edge of a stick to stir the ashes. "Looks like documents. Some pages may have survived." He gestures to Ruiz. "Bag what's left."

As Ruiz begins collecting the charred fragments, Bailey sniffs around the edges of the room. Then, he lets out a sharp bark and darts toward the far wall, nose presses against a gap near the floorboards.

"What is it, boy?" Amelia asks him, crouching next to him.

Bailey paws gently at the boards. Something metallic glints beneath them.

Tom kneels beside them, prying the piece free. It is the corner of small tin box, its sides warped but intact enough to read the faint impression of a stamp: **Maplewood Savings and Loan.**

"The same bank where Eric's safe deposit box is," Amelia whispers.

Tom nods. "And the same place Hank's accounts ran through."

Amelia stands, brushing ash from her hands, and her eyes drift to the wall above the mantle. The old shotgun still hangs, the same one she'd seen the first time she visited the cabin. The stock is worn, the metal dull, but something about it makes her pulse increase.

She steps closer, studying it in the beam of Tom's flashlight. "That gun," she murmurs.

Tom glances over. "What about it?"

"It's been on my mind since we were here last," she explains. "I am not sure what it is yet, but something about it is begging me to figure it out."

Tom crosses the room and reaches up, takes it down carefully. Dust falls from the mount as he eases it free. "You think this could be *the* shotgun?"

Amelia hesitates. "I don't know. But if it is, it's been hanging here for ten years right under everyone's nose and who put it there, obviously not Eric?"

He turns the weapon over in his hands, checking the chamber. "Not loaded. I'll take it in. Maybe we can find out who owns it."

“Good,” Amelia says softly. “Even if it’s nothing, at least it’ll stop whispering at me.”

Lila gives a low whistle. “Only you would get haunted by a firearm.”

“Haunted or not,” her eyes still fixed on the gun, “it’s been waiting for someone to notice it.”

Tom nods, his expression thoughtful as he wraps the shotgun in a spare evidence cloth. “Let’s see what it’s been keeping quiet about.”

Outside, the wind picks up, rattling the loose shutters like a storm beating the cabin.

Lila stands near the door, looking out toward the tree line. “I don’t think this was Jimmy trying to hide evidence,” she says softly. “I think it was someone trying to destroy it.”

“Or both,” Amelia murmurs. “Maybe he got here first, tried to grab something, but someone caught up with him.”

Tom’s face is grim. “Let’s finish the sweep before we lose light.”

They step back outside, Bailey takes the lead again. The ground is uneven, a mix of leaves, broken branches, twigs, and mud. Then Bailey freezes, nose focusing on the ground. He paws, brushing up leaves to get to the mud.

Tom squats next to examine what Bailey is after. “Fresh tire tracks. A truck with wide treads. May be the same pattern as the ones near the Inn last week.”

Bailey trots a few feet farther, barking once more. Near the edge of the clearing, half-buried in leaves, was a lighter—silver, clean, and out of place among the grime.

Tom picks it up carefully. "Recently dropped, it isn't muddy."

"Jimmy's?" Amelia asks.

Tom shakes his head. "I don't recall ever seeing him with this one. This one's newer."

Lila's voice is small. "Then whoever was here came after him."

The woods seem quiet again, the kind of silence that hums louder than noise. Amelia looks around, heart hammering.

"Tom," she says softly, "if someone's been burning evidence, we're getting close to something big."

He nods in agreement. "Too close, maybe."

They fan out for a final sweep. Ruiz flags footprints near the tracks, a volunteer finds a cigarette butt still damp from a recent rain, Amelia spots a scuff in the bark where a vehicle had brushed past. Nothing conclusive, but together, the details seems to paint a picture.

By the time the group makes their way back toward the vehicles, the last streaks of sunset have drained from the sky. Flashlights swing in the dark like fireflies. Ruiz carries the evidence bags, careful with every step.

"Anything else?" Tom asks as they regroup.

"One more thing," Ruiz mentions. "Found these fresh footprints near the tracks. Bigger shoe size, could be a man's. Deep impressions. Whoever it was, they were running."

"Toward or away?"

Ruiz explains. "Away from the cabin, but they stop at the road. Looks like whoever it was had a ride waiting or this Is where the truck was parked."

Tom's face is stern. "All right. We'll have the lab compare tread casts to the ones we pulled from the Inn."

He turns to Amelia and Lila. "You two shouldn't have been out here."

"Maybe not," Amelia replies quietly, "but Bailey led us straight to the truth."

Tom smiles and nods. "He's got a great nose on him."

Tom reaches down and rubs his head. Bailey wags modestly, pleased with the compliment.

Lila rubs her arms. "If this is what a trail gone cold looks like, I'd hate to see one that's hot."

Amelia staring back at the dark outline of the cabin. The chimney smoke has thinned, vanishing into the night sky like a secret trying to escape.

"What now?" she asks softly.

Tom looks down the path, then back toward town. "Now," he replies, "we get answers before someone else disappears."

They start the walk back in a quiet line, boots trampling over dry leaves. The search party peels off toward their trucks, voices low, radios crackling softly in the distance.

Someone hands out bottled waters from a plastic tote; Lila takes one and passes another to Amelia.

"You all right?" Lila asks.

"I will be, when Jimmy is."

By the time the last flashlight blinks out in the woods, the night swallows the color from everything. The search suspends until morning, but the weight of what not yet found travels back to town with them.

The headlights of Tom's SUV cut a clean path through the trees as he opens the back and carefully places the wrapped shotgun inside. He pauses, then clicks the hatch shut with an extra press, as if locking away more than metal.

On the slow drive back from town, Amelia watches the dark blur of branches slide by and thinks about the moments that won't settle: the lighter, the ledger, the lists, the shotgun, the photos, how all those initials, dates, cash and tire tracks stitch together into a net that someone is frantically trying to cut apart.

She glances at Bailey in the rearview mirror. He meets her eyes as if to say, *We're not done.*

No, she thinks to herself. *Not even close.*

They pull up in front of the Inn to the comfort of the porch light and the shape of home. Lila reaches across the console and squeezes Amelia's hand. "Text me if you hear anything. Even if it's just 'I'm okay.'"

"I will," as she returns the squeeze, meaning it.

Lila leans over the seat to scratch Bailey's ears. "Good work, Detective."

Bailey yawns extravagantly, which in Bailey language means, *Thank you, I know.*

The porch light spills a soft circle across the steps as Amelia unlocks the door. Bailey hops through first, nose low, making sure that his home has not changed while they were gone.

Inside, the Inn has settled into evening: a reading lamp in the parlor, the hush of footsteps and muffled voices upstairs.

Amelia pulls out some left overs and places them in the microwave. While they are warming, she gets Bailey his dinner, as he is sitting at attention by his bowls, waiting patiently.

As she sits to eat, she realizes how hungry she is, her mind has been so occupied she didn't notice.

The kettle's whistle rings out as it reaches a boil. Amelia pours hot water over a teabag and wraps her hands around the mug, letting the steam soften the cold in her chest.

"What are we doing?" she whispers, not to give up, only to release the weight of it. Tires slashed. A warning left up close. A hooded figure. A bag of cash and pills. A ledger that should never have existed. A gun that wouldn't stop whispering. Again, her grandmother's words come through loud and clear, to keep her steadfast and resolved. "I know, I need to push on."

The porch light draws a few moths into a quiet orbit. Down the lane, a pair of headlights turn on and stay on, nothing more than neighbors answering the call of supper. One by one, her guests return from their days, wind-pinked cheeks, grateful smiles, stories about antiques and views and the small kindnesses of a town that still remembers how to be one.

She welcomes them with the warmth she always musters, noting who wants tea and who needs an extra blanket, who asks after Bailey and who asks after *her.*

Mr. and Mrs. Kent, bundled against the cold and brimming with curiosity. Behind them, a pair of new arrivals from out of town holding their paper bags from the diner, clearly returning to find out what all the fuss was about.

"Ms. Hartford," Mrs. Kent begins before she is even inside, "we heard at Dottie's that there was a search tonight! For that poor mechanic boy! Did they find him?"

Amelia shakes her head while lowering it a bit. "Not yet. The search was called off for the night, but the Sheriff's team will start again at first light."

"Oh my," Mrs. Kent puts her hand to her chest. "Terrible thing. Ten years ago, that other death, and now this one somehow connected. Gives me chills."

"Or goosebumps," Mr. Kent adds. "Depending on your constitution."

Behind them, the out-of-town couple exchange looks. The man's expression is equal parts concern and excitement. "A real mystery?" he asks. "In Maplewood?"

Lila, never one to let a good rumor go unpolished, smiles knowingly. "You could say that. Though around here, we prefer to call it 'community problem solving.'"

Mrs. Kent gets up close to Amelia. "You're helping again, aren't you? You always seem to be right in the middle of these things."

Amelia hesitates, then offers a small, careful smile. "Only because trouble keeps finding its way to my door."

The room fills with murmurs of concern and speculation as the guests settle in the parlor, chatting in low tones over tea and cookies that Lila manages to "magically" produce. Bailey accepts more than one pat as he makes the rounds, his gentle presence diffusing some of the unease.

Amelia lets them talk for a while, thinking to herself, better to let curiosity have its air than to bottle it up.

Eventually, the guests retreat upstairs one by one, the creak of the staircase and soft murmurs of goodnights carrying through the quiet house.

When the last door closes upstairs, the house exhales its soft goodnight.

In her room, Amelia sets her phone on the nightstand and takes a seat on the edge of the bed, Bailey curls up at her feet. For a moment she just breathes, the way you do when you've made it home and the world has agreed to wait until morning.

The phone buzzes.

She snatches it up. Only a text from Lila: *You okay?*

Amelia smiles and types back: *Yes. Thank you. Sleep.*

She lies down, the day replays behind her eyes: a tin stamped with **Maplewood Savings and Loan** glinting in ash, a lighter winking from leaves, the hush that fell when Tom took the shotgun from the wall.

Bailey sighs himself into dreams. The Inn's old bones creak and settle, a lullaby she's come to love.

"Tomorrow," she tells the quiet room, to herself most of all. "We keep going."

16

Calm Before The Storm

Breakfast is off and running today. Despite yesterday's search, Amelia is back in her rhythm, chatting with the guests and refiling their coffee as she goes. Mrs. Kent stands and walks over to Amelia, cupping her mug as if it could warm the worry from her fingers. "Any news this morning? About the mechanic boy?"

"Sheriff Tom's team went back out at first light," Amelia explains. "If there's news, we'll hear."

The routine is briefly interrupted with the a sudden cold burst of air coming through the front door.

Lila enters the kitchen with her normal cheery spirit and her scarf flying behind her, trying to keep up. She drops her coat on a chair, as she sighs. "If I never see another pine tree in the dark, I'll live a long and happy life."

Amelia manages a weary smile. "You say that now, but give it a week and you'll be planning a 'forest retreat.'"

Lila wags her finger. "Only if the forest comes with central heating and pie delivery."

The guests, very used to her presence, giggle and smile. Mr. Kent offers, "Maybe next time you are on a manhunt you should go better prepared."

"Oh, no, no more manhunts please," Amelia announces while shaking her head and starting up another pot of coffee.

After the guests are done with breakfast and leave for their day, Lila sits her phone on the counter and hits play, as the song "Working Nine To Five" begins. "Here we go, let's clean this place up and get back to work on solving this case."

After her immediate chuckle, Amelia admits, "I don't know what I would I do without you."

They both get to work. As soon as the kitchen is tidy once again, Amelia fills the kettle while Lila fetches two mugs and rummages for the "good tea," the kind she claims is "for guests," but uses whenever comfort is needed.

Bailey curls up in his bed, head resting on his paws, eyes half-closed but ears still twitching. He never really turns off when something is unsettled.

Amelia pours the tea and sinks into a chair across from Lila.

Lila starts, in a soft voice, "So. What do we actually know?"

Amelia rubs her temples, mentally stacking clues like plates that don't quite fit. "We know there was a tin from the bank hidden in the cabin. We know Eric's name shows up in ledgers connected to Hank and Jimmy. We found cash and pills buried behind the cabin, and someone tried to burn more records last night."

"Plus," Lila adds, "the shotgun. Don't forget your haunted gun."

Amelia gives her that look. "I'm not calling it haunted."

Lila grins. "You're *thinking* it."

Amelia sips her tea, letting the warmth steady her. "And, Jimmy is missing. Whatever he knew, whoever he was afraid of... they got to him first."

"Or he's hiding," Lila offers gently. "You said he was scared. Maybe he ran."

"Maybe, but I don't think he'd leave without trying to tell me the truth. He wanted to meet. He sounded desperate."

Amelia moves on, "You know, I've been thinking about that list from the safe deposit box, HR, Marcus, Jimmy, Jonah, Virgil. Everyone but Virgil is either dead, missing, or lying through their teeth. Not a great batting average."

"Let's hope the baker remains the exception. I'm not ready to suspect anyone who makes lemon scones."

Bailey gives a faint whine, as if agreeing that pastries should remain innocent.

"Agreed, we don't want to throw out the sweets if they aren't soured."

Their laughter is tired but real, the kind that cuts through exhaustion and lets relief breathe for a moment.

Lila asks, "Back to the subject, what do we still need?"

"We need to find out who Marcus is or find out what he knows and we need evidence linking one of them to the shotgun that killed Eric."

"Don't forget, we need to figure out if Jimmy lied due to fear or because he has a part in covering up what happened to Eric."

"You're right, of course, we don't know why he lied about barely knowing Marcus when we've seen the pictures at the bar and the waitress who put the two of them together regularly," Amelia agrees.

Amelia loosens up and sits back in her chair with a sigh. "If this keeps up, the Maple Leaf Inn will have its own true crime podcast."

Lila chuckles. "Hosted by Dottie, no doubt. With dramatic readings from the dessert menu."

Bailey perks up, leaves his bed and plops down at Amelia's feet.

The phone rings, Amelia crosses the room and picks it up. "Maple Leaf Inn, this is Amelia."

"Hey," Tom's voice on the line, low and tired. "How are the two of you doing this morning?"

"We are fine. Any word on Jimmy?"

"Not yet. We've got the shotgun logged in and the remains from the fire secured. I'll run the serial numbers in the morning. Maybe we can figure out who it belongs to."

"I think that will tell us something. Let's hope it is a helpful something."

"I know you know this, but just... be careful, all right?"

"I'll be fine," she promises. "We're staying put today. No woods, no cabins, no chasing leads."

From across the room, Lila's voice floats toward the phone. "Careful, Sheriff, too many personal calls, people could start to talk."

Amelia groans. "Ignore her."

Tom's laugh is short and warm. "All right. Try to relax today, both of you."

"You too."

She hangs up and leans against the counter, still smiling faintly.

"You know he heard me," Lila grinning before she finishes, "He didn't deny it."

"Oh stop, we are just becoming friends."

Lila stands, stretching. "Fine, but I expect updates. And if he brings pie next time, I'm officially calling it 'a date.'"

Amelia chuckles and shakes her head as she returns to her chair.

Amelia pulls her phone out as it rings, "Hello."

"Is this Amelia?"

"Yes, it is. Who's this?"

"Hello, this is Stella from the Rusty Anchor. You asked me to call if I thought of anything else."

"Oh, yes, please, what is it?"

"It's Jimmy, he was in here yesterday afternoon, not long, but was in the back office for about twenty minutes and then left."

"Was he okay? People are out looking for him. His garage was broken into and he has been missing for more than twenty-four hours."

"He looked physically fine, but very nervous or maybe scared, since you say there was a break-in. I don't know which, but might be both."

"Thank you for calling me, I will call the Sheriff and let him know. They are back out there today still looking for him."

"Okay, I hope it helps."

"Me too. Take care now."

"You too."

Amelia hangs up the phone and fills Lila in on the call. "I need to call Tom. I can't believe Jimmy was in Brenton when everyone here is frantically looking for him."

"Yes, call him. That is weird, but does Tom know we went to the bar yet?"

"Oh, no, I forgot to tell him. I will save that for later." Amelia hits the number for Tom.

"Hello, is everything okay?" Tom asks.

"Yes, but a waitress from the Rusty Anchor just called, Jimmy was there yesterday afternoon for about twenty minutes, while we were all out looking for him."

"Well at least we know he was alive and apparently not being held by anyone," Tom points out.

"Yes, but she said he was in the back office there doing something and he appeared very nervous or scared, she wasn't sure which."

"Got it, thank you for calling me and not just heading out the door on your own."

"You're welcome, like I said, we are staying in today."

"Good, I better brief the rest of the team. Talk later."

"All right, bye." She ends the calls and grabs for her tea.

Lila stops her, "You need a fresh cup, that can't be warm now." She takes the cup and empties in the sink. She returns and as she is refilling the cup, "I don't get it, he had to know you would be worried when he didn't show up at the diner and he was well enough to go to Brenton—he couldn't pick up the phone and call you?"

"I was thinking the same thing," Amelia says.

Bailey starts scratching at the door. "Sorry, boy, let me get that." She lets Bailey out back.

"He is probably bursting, we are usually out and about by now," Lila offers.

"True, I just haven't paid attention to the time."

Bailey runs around the back, chasing leaves as they blow across the yard. Lila and Amelia watch him, enjoying a peaceful moment of normalcy.

As Amelia opens the door to let Bailey back inside, Lila's phone chimes.

Lila takes a look and then sits down at the table, reading something.

Bailey heads to his water bowl and Amelia takes her seat again.

After a few more moments, Lila looks up. "I love it, want to see my new book cover?"

"Oh yes, I completely forgot you are about to publish another book and I haven't even asked about it."

"Totally okay. Honestly, with all that has been going on, I forgot too," as she holds up her phone to show Amelia the photo of her new book cover.

Our New Puppy by Lila Benson, it reads. "That puppy looks like it could be Bailey's," Amelia remarks.

"I know, he inspired me."

"That is wonderful. I am sure the children who read it will love him and the book."

"I think so, who doesn't love a book about a puppy coming home with them?" They both chuckle.

The distraction has left them both relaxed and refreshed.

"You know, I need to use this time to get things done around here. How about you make calls and fill in Edna and Dottie while I work on changing the beds and the laundry?" Amelia asks.

They both go about their decided tasks, and before they know it, it is time to start dinner.

Amelia returns to the kitchen to find Lila already has the oven preheating and a casserole waiting to go in. "You didn't have to do that."

"I know, but we both need to eat and it was in the freezer, so looked like a great solution."

Amelia agrees, "Yes perfect." She goes to the cupboard to get Bailey's dinner. He perks up the minute she opens the door and sits patiently by his bowl, licking his lips in anticipation.

"Here you go, boy. Eat up!" She pats him on the head and leaves him in peace to finish.

Lila and Amelia take their time to eat a quiet meal and play with Bailey.

Amelia's phone rings; it's Tom. "Hello! Is this news about Jimmy?"

"Not really. We have been unsuccessful. I am calling off the search. I sent a deputy to Brenton and he got no answers, only confirmations that Jimmy was seen there alive. I can't justify the man hours."

"I understand, you did your best. Who knows what he is up to."

"I am hitting the sack early. It has been a long, hard two days."

"Good, sleep well."

"You too, good night."

Lila who is waiting patiently, "Well, what did he say?"

"They confirmed he was at the bar yesterday and so they are calling off the search. Tom's going to bed."

"I am sure they all need sleep, I had it after one afternoon and they have been out there for almost two full days."

Just then, the door opens to low voices, guests returning from their day in town.

"We are beat," Mrs. Kent announces as she and her husband enter the kitchen. "We must have walked the whole town today. Everyone is talking about that poor boy,"

"Have you ladies heard anything new since dinner?" Mr. Kent inquires.

Lila is first to the answer. "Only that Jimmy was seen in Brenton yesterday, while we all thought he could be dead, so Sheriff confirmed it and called off the search."

The other guests come in during the explanation. "Wow, wonder why he didn't contact anyone?" one guest blurts out from the hall.

"Good question," Mr. Kent adds, "and not thoughtful at all. He must be up to something."

"Maybe so, but I will sleep better knowing he isn't laying in a ditch," Mrs. Kent admits.

"Would any of you like any tea or cookies tonight?" Amelia asks.

"I think I speak for all of us," as Mr. Kent looks at the other guests, "when I say, no thank you. We are all turning in early, so you ladies can get a peaceful night's rest." The other guests all smile and nod in agreement and few "Oh yes's" are heard from the hall.

"Well, that is my cue too, I am going to head home and turn in myself," Lila announces as she grabs her coat and makes her way to the door.

"Thank you all. I could use an early night too," Amelia says with a smile.

Everyone heads to their rooms, Amelia secures the front door after Lila leaves.

She dims the lights and climbs the stairs, with Bailey close behind. In her room, she sits on the edge of the bed, thoughts spinning through her head: Jimmy's fear, the burned papers, the mysterious lighter, the gun hanging in the cabin, where is Jimmy, what is he up to, why didn't he call.

Something about it all whispers wrongness, though she can't yet make sense of why or what.

She switches off the lamp and gives Bailey a cuddle and kiss on the head. She lays back, staring at the ceiling in the half-dark. Bailey settles at the end of her bed with a soft sigh; he is halfway to dreams.

"Tomorrow," she whispers, "we'll figure this out. A good night's sleep is exactly what we all need to start anew."

Bailey stirs a bit, thumps his tail once, and the room falls still.

17

Coffee, Clues, and Confessions

By seven-thirty the kitchen is humming. The smell of bacon frying, fresh coffee percolating, and sweet smells escaping the oven only add to the sound of the blueberry pancakes being flipped to perfection. The morning light spills across kitchen, throwing a soft gleam onto the plates and flatware, already set for guests. Bailey patrols with purpose, greeting, supervising, accepting pats as his salary.

From the hall comes the unmistakable sound of Lila in motion, scarf, boots, and her bright cheer. She swoops into the kitchen like a colorful comet. “Okay, status update,” Lila announces, as she snags a strip of bacon. “I have cookies for morale, a notepad for scoops, and a working theory that maple syrup improves crime-solving.”

“Do you have a working theory for donut holes, too?” Mr. Kent teases.

"I contain multitudes," she replies solemnly, then winks at Amelia. "You look like you slept all night. A triumph."

"I think I did actually, a luxury."

They move through the familiar rhythm—refills, seconds, the clink of cutlery. Guests trading theories in low, excited tones, making Amelia think of cicadas on a summer night, constant, harmless, slightly overwhelming. She keeps her answers calm and sparse. Bailey makes rounds, tail swishing, easing the edges on everyone's nerves.

Then, mid-sizzle, Bailey's head snaps up. He pivots toward the foyer with sudden, delightful certainty. In two strides he is at the archway, ears forward, tail slapping the jamb as he flies by.

"Tom?" Amelia murmurs to herself as her heart races a bit.

A second later Sheriff Tom Granger fills the doorway, hat in hand, uniform already dusted from the fields. His smile is brief but warm. "Morning," he says to the room at large.

"Sheriff," choruses three guests in varying registers, as if they'd rehearsed.

Amelia wipes her hands and nods toward the parlor. "Give me one minute to finish the last plates. Lila?"

"I'm hostess-slash-stand-up," Lila replies, sweeping a hand toward the table. "Ask me about my pie-of-the-day routine."

Tom's mouth twitches a bit. "Dangerous offer."

Amelia sets down a final plate, squeezes Lila's shoulder in thanks, and leads Tom into the parlor. The room holds the hush of braided rugs, a low fire, and the morning light. She closes the pocket door halfway; the murmur of breakfast softens to a comfortable blur. Bailey parks himself like a shaggy sentry by Tom's boots.

"You have news?" she asks.

Tom doesn't sit. He pulls a clear sleeve from his folder, the scanned copy of Edna's photo and taps the third face. "The unknown man. We put it through old booking records, his name is Marcus Groves. Arrested for possession with intent in Brenton, old charges, friends in low places. He's local to that bar off County Eleven."

"The Rusty Anchor," Amelia says softly.

Tom nods once. "Also, when I left Edna's motel yesterday, a dark pickup blew through the lot and onto the road. I caught a partial plate: PE2. Cross-checking a few hours later, a truck with PE2 is registered to a Marcus Groves out of Brenton."

He lets that settle. The puzzle pieces nudge closer in Amelia's mind until they touch.

"That explains why he'd be at the bar a lot. But Jimmy, why is *he* in so many photos with Marcus and why is he a regular at the bar in Brenton?"

Tom's gaze sharpens. "Am I missing something?"

She hesitates, then walks over and opens the desk drawer. She pulls out the matchbook, small and guilty against her palm, their first tether to Brenton. She sets it on the parlor table between them.

Tom's face doesn't harden, exactly. His brows rise. "You've had this how long?"

"Since the cabin. Before the case was officially reopened. I didn't know for sure it was anything."

"That's not how this works now that we have a man missing."

"I know." She hears the earnestness in her own voice and, beneath it, the tug-of-war she's been fighting since Edna knocked on her door. "I'm not playing games with you, Tom. I wasn't sure. And I..." She exhales. "I should have turned it over."

He doesn't press the advantage; that isn't his way. He tucks the matchbook into an evidence bag and seals it. "For what it's worth," he starts, softer, "I get why you held back. But going forward, anything, no matter how small, comes to me."

Amelia's eyes rise to his and she nods. "Understood."

Tom studies her, the edge in his posture easing. "You're still holding something."

"I... I... we went to the bar, yesterday. We were careful." She sees the protest rising and cuts it off gently. "I didn't do anything. I just looked."

"At what?" he asks, though she can see he already has a list of things he doesn't want the answer to include.

She pulls out her phone, opens the photos, and hands it to him. "That wall of photos. Regulars. Years of snapshots."

Tom flips through: Eric, Hank, and Marcus in hunting gear. Eric and Jimmy with a deer, the same clothes as the first photo. Then Jimmy and Marcus again, and again, poker nights, bar porch, the kind of permanence that suggests a close friendship or partnership, not a passing acquaintance.

His jaw sets. “And this was yesterday?”

“Lila and Bailey waited outside. A waitress pointed me to the wall. She said Jimmy and Marcus are in once a month, and yes she told me his name was Marcus, but she didn’t know his last name.”

He nods once, tight. “Text these to me.”

She takes her phone back and immediately starts sending them to his phone, the digital pinging of his phone hits a nerve, each time she hits send, confirming why Tom is irritated with her adventure.

Tom slips the folder back beneath his arm, the evidence bagged matchbook now included. “We’ll loop this into the time lines. The plate, the bar, the photos.” He looks at her. “I expect you to stay put today. Do you see why?”

“Yes,” Honesty tugs at the corners of her mouth. “I won’t like it, though.”

“Good, then you’ll really mean it when you try.”

A tiny laugh makes its way out. “I will try.”

Bailey nudges Tom’s knee with a gentle insistence. Tom scratches behind one ear; Bailey closes his eyes in bliss.

“Oh, wait, one more thing,” she adds. “The shotgun. Have you checked the serial number yet?”

“Not yet, heading back there to check in, I know you have some sort of intuition about it. I will let you know as soon as I do.”

From the kitchen, a burst of laughter carries through the half-closed door, followed by Lila's unmistakable, "...and then I said, '*Sir, this is a diner*!'" The sound softens something in both their faces.

Tom sets his hat back on, balancing duty with the softness of homey noise and coffee and a dog who has clearly adopted him. "Stay here today," he reminds her, already stepping toward the foyer. "Let me work the angles that require a badge."

Amelia walks him to the door. "You'll call, whatever you find, or with news on Jimmy?"

"I will." He pauses, eyes catching hers for a half-breath longer than necessary. "And Amelia? Thanks for the photos."

"Thanks for the warning," smiling despite herself.

He tips the brim and is gone, boots on the hardwood, the front door's low thump, Bailey's tail thudding the baseboard like an echoing promise.

A heartbeat later, Lila flies into the parlor as if she were on wheels. "Spill," her eyes wide. "He had that look. The something happened or found out look."

Amelia lifts her brows. "Marcus Groves. Brenton. Old drug charges. The truck at Edna's motel? Partial plate PE2. Matches Marcus." She places her hand on her hip, "And I gave him the matchbook."

Lila's mouth drops open with scandalized delight. "You confessed? Without an attorney present?"

"I texted him the bar photos." Amelia sinks into the chair, a pile of weight and relief balancing in her chest.

Lila perches on the armchair like an exclamation mark. “Which means...”

“Which means this Marcus guy, who is obviously tied to them all, is a bad guy.” Amelia rubs her thumb along her palm. “Jimmy must have called me because something finally outweighed his fear. And now...” She can’t finish.

Lila’s face softens. “We’ll find him. Also, this is not your fault, he could have told us who Marcus really was when we asked, maybe even gone to the Sheriff himself.”

Amelia nods, letting the words land like a stone in calm water—sinking, settling, true. From the kitchen, plates clink; someone asks for the recipe for the house granola; Bailey returns to rest his head on her knee, asking nothing, offering everything.

“Okay,” Lila perks up but businesslike. “Today we play it Tom’s way. We stay put, but we keep our phones on, and we don’t do anything brave or daring without his say-so.”

“That last one was aimed at me,” Amelia says dryly.

“I have no idea what you mean,” as she rolls her eyes and grins. “I’ll charm the guests and keep the rumor mill from spontaneously combusting. You... sit, breathe, and pretend to enjoy being told what to do by a handsome authority figure.”

Amelia laughs, the sound loosens something tight in her chest. “Go supervise the coffee, you menace.”

“As you wish,” she flies out, just as she entered.

Amelia stands, crosses to the window, and lets her gaze drift over the front walk to the line of trees beyond. Late-autumn light makes lacework of the remaining leaves. Somewhere out there, answers move in their own patterns, slower than fear wants, surer than doubt believes.

Her phone buzzes: a text from Tom: *Thank you again. Stay put.* A second later, another: *We'll find him.*

She types back: *We're here. We'll be waiting.*

Bailey shifts at her side, warm and constant. She rests a hand on his head and lets the morning carry on around them. The clatter, the chatter, the ordinary courage of a town that keeps showing up.

Staying put is tough, when deep down she wants to head out and help. But, for now, it will have to be enough.

18

Stranger Danger

By midmorning, the breakfast rush has tapered off to the quiet rhythm Amelia loves, dishes stacked neatly in the drying rack, the low tick of the kitchen clock, sunlight spilling across the worn pine floors. The Inn smells faintly of cinnamon and coffee, warm and content, like the world has finally remembered how to exhale.

Lila is perched on a stool, tying her scarf for the third time and pretending to be helpful. "If Tom texts again, tell him I've filed a formal complaint about this whole *stay put* policy. It's bad for morale."

Amelia smiles faintly as she wipes down the counter. "I'll forward that to the Sheriff's Department's suggestion box."

Bailey lifts his head from his usual post by the back door. His ears pop up, straight, his entire body goes rigid. The sudden growl that rolls up from his chest makes the hair rise on Amelia's arms.

"Bailey? What is it boy?"

He is already moving, heading toward the front of the house, his nose in the air leading the way, tail low and stiff. Amelia and Lila follow, through the foyer and over to the big bay window overlooking the gravel road.

A man stands near the edge of the property line. Hood up, shoulders square, hands buried in his jacket pockets. Even at that distance, a chill rolls down her neck and out her arms, not just out of place, but deliberate. Watching.

Lila whispers, "Well, either he's lost... or we might make the evening news."

Bailey's growl deepens. The man shifts, half-turning as if to look straight through the window at them. The sunlight catches on something slung over his shoulder, long, metal, unmistakable.

A rifle.

Lila's voice barely above a whisper. "Looks like Tom was right. We might actually be in danger."

Amelia's pulse kicks up a notch. The man lingers a beat too long, then turns and walks down the road, his stride unhurried, vanishing beyond the bend where the trees stand close to one another.

Amelia doesn't waste a second. She grabs her phone and hits Tom's number. "Sheriff, it's Amelia..."

He responds to the tone in her voice. "What's wrong?"

"Someone was standing out front," she explains. "Hooded jacket, tall, rifle on his shoulder. He was watching the Inn. He just walked off down the road and into the trees."

"Stay inside and lock up, away from the windows," Tom orders sharply. "I'm two minutes out."

The call drops.

Lila moves to the door, flipping the locks while Bailey stations himself in front of the window, a low rumble vibrating from his chest like a warning that won't end.

"Why does trouble always come to *your* front door?" as Lila tugs the curtain closed. "It's like it has a GPS setting."

"Maybe it likes my coffee," as she tries to lighten the mood, though her hands tremble. "Or, maybe it's your commentary?"

The distant sound of sirens rise over the trees. Bailey's tail starts to wag, his body alert but calmer now. A moment later, the crunch of tires on gravel and the flash of red and blue lights washing over the front porch.

Finally, a firm familiar knock.

Amelia cracks the door open enough to see Tom's face, eyes sharp, jaw set. "You okay?"

"We're fine," as she steps back to let him in. Bailey relaxes instantly, pressing against Tom's leg in recognition.

Tom gives him a distracted pat while scanning the windows. "We saw no one on the way in. He must've had a car or truck parked out of sight in the trees and took off once you spotted him."

He nods to the deputy who had followed him in. "Ruiz, I will stay here with them while you check the perimeter."

Lila frowns. "You mean *we're* staying inside while you do the dangerous part."

Tom doesn't even blink. "That's the arrangement."

Ruiz slips outside, and a few moments later, his voice comes through the radio clipped to Tom's shoulder. "Footprints along the ditch. Headed east. I'll have the rest of the rotation sweep both directions."

"Copy that," Tom replies. He turns back to Amelia and Lila. "I'm assigning deputies in shifts to keep a presence here until we get this under control. Nobody leaves the property alone."

Lila crosses her arms. "Define 'alone.' If I go out with Bailey, does that count?"

"Yes," Tom says flatly. "You don't go anywhere without a deputy."

She sighs. "You're no fun when you're in protective mode."

"Not trying to be fun." His tone softens a hair. "Trying to keep you all breathing."

Lila mutters, "Romantic in a gruff sort of way."

Tom pretends not to hear. He looks back to Amelia. "I'm also moving Edna here from the motel. Too isolated over there. You have room?"

Amelia responds immediately with a nod. "Of course. She can take the south room upstairs. It's quiet."

"Good. I'll have someone bring her over." He hesitates, then adds, "Call her now. Let her know what's happening so she doesn't panic when the car shows up."

Amelia nods again and reaches for her phone. As she dials, Lila leans close to Tom. "You know, I was joking about moving in earlier, but I have the feeling you're about to make it official."

"I am," he states simply. "You're both safer here."

Lila smirks. "Well, Sheriff, next time you want a slumber party, you could just say so."

He gives her a look, irritation or perhaps slight amusement. "Ruiz will drive you to your house so you can pack a bag. Essentials only, let's not make this a day-long affair."

"Do scarves count as essentials?"

"I'm not answering that," as he obviously prohibits a smile from forming. "Let's move."

By the time Lila leaves with Ruiz, the Inn feels both fuller and emptier, energy buzzing under its cozy skin. Amelia finishes her call with Edna, who takes the news with surprising calm.

"I'll pack a small bag," Edna says. "And tell the Sheriff I'd rather be where Bailey is, anyway. He's better than a guard dog—he's family."

When the call ends, Amelia turns to find Tom standing by the window, one hand on the curtain, scanning the road again. His shoulders are tight, the way they get when he is thinking too many steps ahead.

"You sure you're okay?" he asks without turning.

"I'm more worried about Edna," Amelia replies. "She's been through enough."

"She's on her way with Deputy Carlson. He'll bring her straight here."

She nods, glancing toward the coffeepot on the counter. "You want a cup while we wait?"

His lips quirk, a fraction of ease breaking through the tension. "Is that a rhetorical question?"

"Always." She pours two mugs and carries them to the parlor. Bailey follows close, toenails clicking softly on the floor. Outside, a deputy's car idles near the lane, headlights scanning the empty road.

They sit opposite each other, steam curling between them, the sound of the house settling into quiet vigilance. For a long moment, neither speaks.

Finally, Tom says, "I know this is a lot. I didn't want it to get this serious."

"It was already serious," Amelia admits gently. "You just made it official."

He looks up at her, the faintest trace of wryness in his eyes. "I suppose I did."

Bailey stretches out between them with a sigh, his head on his paws, content as if the world hadn't narrowed to shadows and rifle sights.

"You'll let me know the minute you hear something?" Amelia asks.

"I promise, and you'll let me know if that gut of yours tells you anything else. I've learned to trust it, even when it scares me."

She smiles faintly, warming her hands around her cup. "Then we're even."

The crunch of tires on gravel draw both their gazes toward the window. A deputy's car rolls up, headlights washing across the porch. A moment later comes the sound of a door opening, a gentle voice outside, and then the steady tap of shoes on the front steps.

Tom rises. "That'll be Edna."

⁂

Ten minutes later, Edna is sitting in the parlor with a cup of tea between her palms, her overnight bag resting at her feet. She looks smaller in the chair but not fragile, more like someone who has already made peace with fear and simply refuses to yield to it again.

"I hope this isn't too much trouble," as she looks up from her tea at Amelia.

"Not at all," with her reassuring smile. "The Inn's seen more excitement than it ever bargained for lately, but it's still good at what it does, keeping people safe."

Tom stands near the door, scanning his notes, making additions. "I'll post another car out front after dark. I want at least one deputy on watch at all times."

Lila's voice echoes from the foyer as she comes back through the door, a duffel slung over her shoulder and Ruiz trailing behind. "Well, here we are. The Maple Leaf Safehouse! I call dibs on the room with the best lighting."

Tom looks ready to protest, but Lila waves him off. "Kidding. Mostly."

He pinches the bridge of his nose. "No freelancing. No wandering off. Lock the doors, close the curtains, and stay alert."

"Yes, Dad," Lila says sweetly.

He gives her the kind of look that could silence half a town meeting, but she only smiles wider.

Amelia catches the exchange; her heart lightens by the absurd normalcy of it. Even in the middle of danger, Lila can find a joke, and Tom is able to care enough to scold her.

When Tom finally turns toward the door, Amelia follows him to the porch. "Be careful, okay?" she asks of him.

He nods, the porch light catches the faint stubble on his jaw and the weariness under his eyes. "I always am."

"Liar," she says as she shakes her head.

A shadow of a smile tugs at his mouth. "Fine. I'll try harder."

She watches until his car disappears down the lane, the sound of the engine fades away. Behind her, the Inn is alive with the gentle hum of voices, Lila's chatter, Edna's calm tones, and the familiar click of Bailey's nails on the floor.

The old house has never felt more like a refuge or more like a fortress.

Amelia takes one last look at the empty road, then closes the door and locks the bolt. "All right, Grandma," she murmurs under her breath. "If you're watching, wish us luck."

Bailey leans against her leg, solid and steady, the quiet guardian.

19

Cracks in the Armor

By afternoon, the news has moved faster than a November wind: the Maple Leaf Inn is under police watch. A deputy's cruiser idles at the lane; another patrols the side streets. It is a bit surreal, rather than menacing, as Amelia keeps herself busy, between tidying up and chatting with her forced house guests.

Amelia heads to the door, following Bailey, who is already on the run, tail wagging, which sets Amelia's heart at ease. Sure enough, all safe. Dottie arrives exactly as one comes to expect: hip first through the door, paper sacks looped over her arms, chin high with purpose and curiosity.

"Special delivery," she announces, sweeping into the kitchen like she owns shares. "A couple chicken salads, a ham-on-rye, and a couple turkey clubs, one heroic tub of potato salad, and a generous side of local intelligence." She sets the bags down and lowers her voice for effect. "Don't tell the mayor; he thinks intel comes in binders."

Amelia smiles as she wraps her arm around Dottie's shoulders. "Hi, Dottie."

"Hi yourself," already unloading sandwiches onto plates as if the Inn were just another booth at the diner. "Now, my scoop. Hank Ross is everywhere this morning. I've seen him glad-handing like it's an election year. His hands are shaking like a leaf in a thunderstorm. Asking after 'how folks are doing,' like he didn't forget what that meant for a decade."

Amelia trades a look with Lila, who perches on the stool nearest the coffee pot, like it is a throne. "Friendly Hank," Lila remarks. "Now there's an oxymoron."

"Mark my words," Dottie adds, tapping the counter for emphasis, "when a man who never apologizes starts smiling too much, he's either selling a timeshare or hiding a mess."

Before Amelia can reply, Bailey races to the door and she hurries to catch up. She unlocks the bolt and opens the door. Tom steps in, hat tucked under his arm. Amelia invites him to follow toward the kitchen and closes the door, behind him. As they enter the kitchen, his eyes take a quick sweep and land on Dottie with inevitable resignation.

"Tell me those lunches are for the people under my protection," he says.

"And for you if you play nice," Dottie shoots back. "You look hungry."

Tom's mouth stiffens a bit as he shakes his head. "I'll take that under advisement." He turns to Amelia and Lila. "Update: I've got records showing Hank made multiple drug charges on Marcus Groves' record disappear a few years back. Not one; several. Quiet dismissals, 'evidence issues,' and a particularly creative use of 'community service' that never got served."

Lila lets out a low whistle. "So Hank did favors for Marcus. And Marcus... returned them."

"That's the working theory," Tom admits. "It strengthens motive and relationship. Still doesn't tell me where Jimmy is, or what he knows."

From the foyer comes the clack of the front latch and the murmur of Deputy Ruiz's voice, "I'm here."

Dottie waves to everyone and as she passes Ruiz in the hall, "Hi, darling. Bye, darling. The dinner prep calls. If anyone throws a brick, you throw it back."

"Please don't," Tom chimes in automatically.

Dottie hollers back at him. "Figure of speech, Sheriff. Mostly." She swings her coat over her back as she is rushing out the door.

Tom turns to Ruiz. "You take the first shift in the car out front. Log all comings and goings. If anyone lingers on the road longer than they need to tie a shoe, I want a plate and a direction."

"Copy," Ruiz says, already moving back toward the door.

Tom following. He looks back to Amelia, softer now. "I know I'm being... directive."

"You mean bossy?" Lila offers.

"Command-driven," Tom corrects holding back a smile. Then, to Amelia, again: "I'm sorry it has to be like this. The investigation's moving, but we're behind on one very important thing. Jimmy's still missing."

"I know," Amelia agrees, feeling the words like grit behind her ribs. "We'll help however we can."

Edna appears from the staircase. "Thank you," as she addresses all of them, "It is... easier to breathe here."

"Tea helps with that too," Lila chimes in as she pours a cup and signals her to come over where lunch awaits. "You missed Dottie, she brought us all sandwiches and potato salad."

Edna heads toward the table, "And where is Bailey, that four-legged hero?" She glances around.

At the sound of his name, Bailey trots over and rubs his head against Edna's hand. She exhales, smiles, and gives him a few long stokes and a couples pats on the head, as she grabs something from her pocket. "Here you go, boy," handing him a treat she brought along. Bailey sits, takes the treat, and carries it to his bed to enjoy.

"Well, I can see you are all doing just fine, so I am heading back out," Tom announces as he gives a wave, which they all return and he heads to the door. Amelia follows and locks the door behind him.

They settle around the kitchen table, Amelia, Lila, and Edna, while a deputy's silhouette looms comfortably at the edge of the front window like a promise.

Amelia suddenly pushes her plate aside. "I'll be back in a few minutes." She disappears to the office, prints the photos from her phone, and returns with a neat stack still warm from the printer.

She returns to the table, setting the stack down where her plate had been, "Let's lay it out."

They work like quiltmakers piecing a pattern. At the top: the scan of Edna's photograph—Eric, Hank, Marcus in hunting gear. Below it: the Rusty Anchor wall snaps Amelia had taken—Eric and Jimmy beside a deer in the same clothes and hats, then a run of bar photos where Jimmy and Marcus appear again and again. In the margin: a photocopy of Jonah's ledger page with **H.R.** circled in red, and a sheet of Edna's bank records noting unlabeled cash deposits and transfers. Off to the side: the hand-scribbled list found in the safe deposit box—**HR, Marcus, Jimmy, Jonah, Virgil.**

"Oh, Edna, we haven't told you, the mystery man is Marcus Groves, a criminal according to Tom and obviously someone they all knew," Lila explains as she points him out in the photos.

"Yes, all these guys are together constantly in these bar shots," Amelia adds. "A waitress at the bar says Jimmy and Marcus come there every month, together."

"I hope that means we are getting closer to the truth," Edna replies.

"I think so, Tom also told us Hank dismissed Marcus' drug charges more than once. There is a tight connection there."

"Add the money," Lila reminds, sliding the ledger closer. "Hank and Jimmy in Jonah's secret accounts; Eric moving cash like a man trying to get free; drugs and cash buried behind the cabin; another in the bank box. It's all the same river."

Edna's eyes soften with something between grief and clarity. "He was trying to get out. He was stealing from or working with bad men and trying to outrun them."

"Which gives Hank a reason to make this mess disappear," Lila comments. "And Marcus a reason to help."

"All of which gives us a reason to be careful," Amelia admits, the picture tightening in her mind like a net.

Time thins, then thickens again. The deputy's radio crackles and quiets; a pair of guests tiptoe through the hall and, seeing the kitchen table, retreat with wide eyes and whispering good-lucks. Outside, the November sun drifts west; inside, the kettle sings and the potato salad somehow vanishes.

When they finally lean back, the table looked like a small-town evidence board: photographs, initials, arrows drawn in pencil where belief became tentative proof.

Lila checks the clock and blinks. "We've been at this for three hours."

Amelia rubs the smudge of toner from her thumb. "It feels like ten minutes."

Edna reaches across and touches Amelia's hand. "Thank you, for seeing him. Not just his mistakes."

Before Amelia can answer, Bailey's ears spring up. He launches to his feet, nails clicking, tail pounding, thump-thump against the cabinet. A knock, firm but not urgent, sounds at the front door.

"Friend," Lila guesses, reading Bailey's wag like a code.

Amelia stands, feeling the prickle of that fragile line between safety and danger hum against her skin. She takes a look at the table, leaves it as is, and turns for the door.

"Stay," she tells Bailey gently. He sits, patient, pleased, expectant.

She crosses the foyer, the old boards whispering under her steps, and reaches for the latch.

When she opens the door, the afternoon light leans in around a familiar silhouette. Bailey, from the kitchen doorway, gives an approving *woof*, as if to say: *It's okay. This one's ours.*

20
Breaking Point

Standing at the door, not one but three familiar faces: Helen Carver from the Maplewood Motel, Ruth Lane from the rotary committee, and Mrs. Ellis, who runs the church quilting circle. Among them, an assortment of covered dishes, put together like peace offerings.

"Helen," Amelia says, as her head tilts and forehead crinkles. "What's all this?"

Helen smiles, shy but firm. "The town was talking over lunch," she begins. "And well, we decided it wasn't right that you folks are holed up here. So, we brought you dinner."

"Oh my," Amelia steps off to the side signaling them to file inside.

Mrs. Ellis, walks into the hall, lifting her dish as proof. "Chicken and rice casserole. My mother's recipe. It's comfort food. It doesn't fix everything, but it fills the cracks."

Ruth follows and adds, "Blackberry cobbler, still warm. And don't think for a second I'd let you get through a crisis without dessert." She nods toward Helen, who gestures to her own dish. "Green bean casserole. The good kind, with the crunchy onions."

For a moment, Amelia is silent. The simple generosity catches in her throat.

"That's so kind of you," she manages. "You didn't need to do all this."

The women make it into the kitchen, the smell of casseroles and cobbler instantly softening the edges of the long day. Helen looks around, noticing the table full of pictures and papers. "We can't stay," she says gently. "But the town's on your side. We all want you safe. It is obvious you may be stationary but you're still on the case."

Amelia raises a hand to her heart. "Thank you. You have no idea how much it means."

"Don't you worry," Mrs. Ellis says, setting the casserole on the counter with a decisive clatter. "Maplewood looks after its own."

They leave as quickly as they'd come, their kindness lingering like the scent of baked fruit. When the door closes behind them, Amelia turns to Lila and Edna with tears shining faintly in her eyes.

"Well," Lila speaks up, hands on her hips, "if I die tonight, I'll die stuffed and sentimental."

Edna smiles. "It's something, isn't it? After all that's happened, people still find ways to be kind."

Amelia nods, her voice steady again. "It's exactly what Grandma loved about this town."

"Time for a break, let's move to the counter, with the food," as Lila heads to the cabinet to retrieve plates.

They gather around the counter, each claiming a stool, the dishes spread before them like a feast. Bailey sits patiently beside his bowl, tail sweeping the floor. Amelia dishes out a scoop of chicken and rice for him before serving the others.

The first bite is pure comfort. The tension of the last few days seems to ease under the simple rhythm of passing plates and soft conversation. The evening falling, as it always does.

"I should be scared," Lila admits, licking cobbler filling from her spoon, "but between this food, Bailey, and the sheriff's watchful eye, I think I'm feeling downright optimistic."

Edna nods. "The whole town looking out for us, the sheriff's on board, Bailey's sharp ears, how could we not feel safe?"

Bailey thumps his tail, licking a bit of rice from his muzzle.

Later, as the last of the dishes are scraped clean and stacked in the sink, a few guests pass through the kitchen on their way to bed, lingering in the doorway with hesitant smiles.

"Big crowd outside tonight," one said. "Two patrol cars, I think. You're famous again, Ms. Hartford."

Another adds, "Don't worry. We told Dottie that you're all under *protective custody*, not *suspicion*." He grins. "She's spinning it into next week's gossip already."

Lila laughs. “Excellent. Maybe she'll promote Bailey to full deputy.”

When the guests drift off, the house settles into its night-time rhythm. Distant owls hooting to find a mate, the faint hum of a police radio from outside, the creak of old timbers. It starts to feel like the worst has passed.

Amelia's phone buzzes on the counter; it's Tom.

“Hey,” she answers softly, stepping away from the sink.

“Hey yourself,” his voice, low and tired. “Still quiet there?”

“Quiet as a church mouse, dinner arrived courtesy of the good women of Maplewood. I think half the town is feeding us by proxy.”

He chuckles under his breath. “I should've known they'd rally. No word on Jimmy yet. We're widening the search grid tomorrow.”

“I'm sorry, I wish I could help.”

“You already are, just stay safe tonight. Promise me.”

“I promise,” she agrees. “We're heading to bed soon.”

“Good. Maybe tomorrow brings something better.”

“I'll hold you to that. Good night,” as she experiences the warmth of his voice, which lingers longer than the line itself.

Before dawn, noise interrupts the quiet, first a powerful “pop” from outside which arouses Bailey into a sharp continuous bark, then moments later, a loud pounding beneath them. Bailey becomes more insistent. Amelia shoots upright in bed, heart instantly pounding out of her chest.

"Bailey?" she gasps, as she jumps up to her feet. She throws open the bedroom door and he is down the hall and halfway down the stairs before she makes it to the top, his claws skittering across the wood. Other bedrooms are opening and guests peering out to see what is happening.

The sound loud again but clearer, a desperate thumping against the back door.

Amelia runs, robe flying, hair loose, cold air stinging her bare feet as she reaches the kitchen. Bailey is ahead of her, growling low, hackles up. Through the window, a shape leans against the frame, slumped, half-collapsed.

She unlocks the door and starts to open it, his weight taking over, she lets go of the door to catch him as he falls inside.

"Jimmy!" she cries out.

He is pale, sweat slicking his forehead, one leg soaked in blood. His fingers claw weakly at the doorframe. "He knows... I talked," he rasps. "He knows."

"Sit, no, here, lie down." Amelia lowers him to the floor, grabbing a towel from the counter and pressing it to the wound. Bailey whines beside her, hovering like a shadow.

Lila's footsteps pound down the stairs. "Oh my God—Jimmy!"

Edna appears behind her, eyes wide, robe clutched tight.

Deputy Ruiz bursts through the door a heartbeat later, weapon drawn, his face set. "Everyone, get back—get down!" He kneels beside Amelia, takes one look at Jimmy, and shouts into his radio, "Need an ambulance to the Maple Leaf Inn... gunshot victim, alive, hurry!"

Amelia barely hears him over the rush of her own pulse. She presses harder on Jimmy's leg, whispering, "Stay with us. You're safe now, okay? You made it."

Jimmy's lips move, but the sound was too faint to catch. His eyes flutter.

Then his head rolls weakly toward Amelia. "Eric... he was gonna tell. Hank, Hank and Marcus, Eric was going to expose them. They're after me now."

Before Amelia can answer, a loud sharp *crack* tore through the woods, a gunshot, echoing like thunder through the night.

Lila screams. Bailey lunges toward the back door, barking furiously. Outside, a deputy's radio flares to life.

"Shots fired! Rear of the Inn!"

Lila kneels beside them, tears streaking her face. "We've got you, Jimmy. Hang on."

Sirens wail in the distance, growing louder. Ruiz rises and sprints back outside, shouting orders to the other deputies.

Moments later, headlights wash over the kitchen walls as the ambulance pulls around the backside of the Inn. Paramedics rush in, voices sharp and focused. They take over for Amelia, as one applies pressure, while the other checks his vitals. Almost in an instant, they lift Jimmy onto a stretcher and announce that they are taking him to the hospital. Amelia stands back, frozen but also shaking, her hands and robe streaked with blood she hadn't noticed until now.

Outside, the ambulance door slams shut, the engine gains momentum, and the siren fades off toward town, silence falls on the Inn.

Five minutes later, Tom arrives, hair uncombed, uniform half-buttoned, eyes burning with fury and worry all at once. He doesn't speak, he visually checks each of them with a soldier's precision: Edna's trembling hands, Lila's tears, the blood on Amelia's robe.

"Is everyone okay?" his voice taut.

Amelia nods. "We're fine. But Jimmy... he said Hank and Marcus killed Eric. He said they're after him now."

Tom exhales sharply, gripping the back of a chair until his knuckles turn white. "They just tried to finish the job."

He looks toward the window, the darkness beyond. "No one goes outside. Not tonight. Not until I say so."

Amelia's voice is quiet but certain. "Tom, something's off about all of this. Something doesn't add up."

"Like what?"

She glances toward the trees, the cold light edging the horizon. "I don't know. But something about this, it's just wrong, Jimmy's words maybe? What was the second shot for —Jimmy was already inside and it sounded farther away than the shot which woke us. I'm done sitting on the sidelines."

Tom turns toward her, frowning, ready to argue, but the steeliness in her eyes stops him.

She wipes her hands on the towel, straightens herself, and looks out into the dim dawn. The woods stare back, still and silent, holding the secrets of men who thought they'd buried them deep.

"Whatever it is, Amelia," he says softly as he puts his arm around her shoulders, "we'll find it." She nods against his arm.

Bailey stands beside her, head high, tail still, as the first sunlight spills over the Inn. It is the beginning of another day.

By now, guests are gathering near the kitchen. "I am so sorry for your abrupt awakening, so early," Amelia addresses her guests.

"I can't speak for everyone, but this doesn't look like you caused it. We're fine," Mr. Kent replies and the others nod in agreement.

"I will get the coffee started. I don't think any of us are falling back asleep anytime soon," Lila tells them as she is already pouring the grinds in.

"Sounds like just what we all need," Tom says, as he guides Amelia away from the crowd into the parlor, "Thank you, Lila."

Lila waves him off and continues her quest, "Attention everyone, we are going to need to clean up in here, so find a spot in the library and I will bring the coffee and fixings as soon as they're ready."

Edna stays behind to assist, the others turn and head toward the library, whispering to one another as they go.

Deputy Ruiz returns to the kitchen with a camera and begins taking shots of the scene, the door, the floor, the steps outside, the backyard. Edna and Lila watch him, diligently record everything while they await the coffee.

"Deputy, I am leaving you a cup here on the counter when you have a minute, we're heading to the library with the guests," Lila says and she and Edna carry the trays with coffee, cream, sugar, and mugs to the library.

As they leave, a voice comes through the walkie, "We haven't found anyone, have one report about a mile away of a truck driving fast down the lane about an hour ago, but that's it."

Deputy Ruiz replies, "Thanks. One of you head to the hospital and stay with Jimmy Dale, just in case."

The voice chimes back, "Got it, I'll head there now, about five minutes away."

Meanwhile, in the parlor, "Seriously, are you all right?" Tom asks.

Amelia looks at him, pauses a moment, "Yes, I am, but I am troubled by all this."

"I completely understand, you should be, this is not what anyone wants to wake up to."

"It's not just that, a loud shot rings out waking us, Jimmy shows up, apparently after running with what looks like a bullet wound in his leg. Then, after he is safely inside, another shot is fired from some distance away." Amelia rubs her hand down her head, across her mouth and chin. "It doesn't make sense. How does a wounded man flee a gunman to that degree, and why was the first shot louder and feel closer than the second, and what or who was the second shot for?"

"I guess I will have to take your word for that. I wasn't here when all that took place, but I can see how it seems off to you now. I am sure my deputies will have more information and maybe can fill in the details. They were all outside or in their cars when the shots were fired."

"That's not all, why didn't he say who shot him? He tells me Hank and Marcus killed Eric, but not who shot him. Wouldn't that be the first thing you tell someone when you are bleeding on their floor?"

"I can't answer that either, maybe that was more on his mind. The last time you spoke he wanted to tell you something. Perhaps that is what it was and so that was first thing on his mind, telling you that."

"Maybe, I guess we will see." Amelia lets it rest, but it still weighs heavy on her mind. "I know you need to get to the hospital to question him. So you should go; we'll be fine here."

Tom agrees and she walks him to the door. "I'll be back later to check in with you, all of you," Tom says as he walks out.

Amelia locks the door and heads to the kitchen, Bailey still close, her shadow.

"Miss Hartford," Ruiz greets her as she enters, "I am almost done here, I have called in for some cleaners, they are on their way."

"Thank you, I am going to get breakfast started over here." Amelia begins unloading ingredients from the fridge, turns on the oven, and grabs the muffin pans from the cabinet.

"What are you doing?" Lila exclaims as she returns to the kitchen.

"Getting breakfast going, I have guests to feed." She keeps her attention on her measuring and mixing.

"You need a minute more. I am sure your guests will understand. Why don't you go upstairs and change and clean up?" Lila urges.

Amelia looks down, "Oh, you're right. I still have Jimmy's blood on me."

"Good—you go do that, I will start the breakfast and you can join in when you get back." Lila grabs a pan and bacon and gets to work.

Amelia stops and turns before heading to the stairs, "How are the guests doing?"

"They are all in the library, enjoying their coffee and sharing theories and speculations as we speak. I'd say they are doing just fine." Lila smiles as she places her hand on Amelia's arm. "I am pretty certain they are working on their stories for when they head home, more excitement than they paid for, for sure."

Amelia, sighs and cracks a small smile as she heads to her room, as Bailey falls in behind her.

21

Whispers in the Hospital

By late morning, the Maple Leaf Inn has settled into its quiet rhythm.

The last of the breakfast dishes are drying in neat rows along the counter, sunlight glinting off the clean China. Amelia wipes down the table one final time, the hum of normalcy doing its best to soothe the knot in her stomach. Bailey lies stretched across his blanket near the window, one ear twitching in his sleep.

Edna sits in the parlor with a mug of tea clasped between both hands, her shoulders slumped in exhaustion. She pulls herself to her feet. "I think I'm going to lie down for a bit," she says softly. "Just for an hour."

Amelia's gaze softens. "That's a good idea. Lila and I are going to go to the hospital. We'll be back before you know it."

Edna hesitates, then nods. “Be careful. Both of you.”

“We always are,” Lila says, though her eyes flick toward Amelia, knowing full well that’s only half true.

Once Edna disappears upstairs, Amelia grabs her coat and keys. “Let’s go see Jimmy.”

Bailey lifts his head, hopeful.

“Not this time,” Amelia murmurs, scratching behind his ears. “Guard duty.”

Bailey huffs but settles back down, resigned.

The hospital smells like antiseptic and old coffee—clean but tense, as though the walls themselves know secrets are being whispered inside them.

Jimmy Dale’s room is at the end of the hall.

A deputy stands outside the door, his posture stiff, eyes alert. He nods when he sees Amelia. “Sheriff’s orders. No visitors without approval.”

“He’s expecting us,” Amelia announces.

The deputy glances at his clipboard, then steps aside. “Five minutes.”

Inside, Jimmy looks smaller than Amelia remembers. His leg is wrapped in thick bandages, color drained from his face. His eyes dart to the door the moment they enter.

“You shouldn’t be here,” he mutters.

“That’s funny,” Lila replies, folding her arms. “You sent for us.”

Jimmy swallows hard. "I didn't think the sheriff would be watching me like a hawk."

Amelia pulls a chair closer to the bed and sits. "Jimmy... someone shot you."

His breath shudders. "I know."

"Who did it?"

His eyes flick away. "I didn't see them."

Lila scoffs. "Where were you? Did someone do a drive-by shooting?"

Jimmy presses his lips together, knuckles whitening against the blanket. "It happened fast. I heard movement. Then pain. That's all."

Amelia studies him, the fear, the guilt etched deep into his face. "You don't sound like someone who's telling the whole truth."

Jimmy lets out a shaky laugh. "That's because the whole truth gets people killed."

Silence settles between them.

Amelia reaches into her bag and pulls out a photograph, the one Edna showed them. She lays it gently on the bed.

Jimmy's breath catches.

"Did you take this picture?" Amelia asks.

He nods. "Yeah. We went deer hunting together every year. Me, Eric, Hank... Marcus sometimes."

"Marcus Groves," Lila says flatly.

Jimmy nods again. "They were thick as thieves back then."

Amelia's voice stays calm. "The gun in the cabin. You told Tom it wasn't Eric's."

"It's mine," Jimmy blurts out. "I never said it wasn't. I just...I left it there, I couldn't go back. After Eric died, hunting lost its appeal."

Lila leans forward. "Funny how your gun ends up in the cabin where Eric was staying and the gun he supposedly shot himself with never made it to evidence."

Jimmy's face twists. "You think I did it?"

"I think you know who did," Lila snaps.

Jimmy's eyes fill. "I always knew. I just never thought they'd turn on me."

Amelia's heart thuds. "Jimmy... did Hank Ross and Marcus Groves kill Eric?"

He nods once. Barely.

"They were into something big," he whispers. "Smuggling. Payoffs. Eric wanted out. He was scared. Said Hank was too close to the wrong people."

"That's why he wrote the letter," Amelia says softly.

Jimmy's shoulders sag. "I warned him. I told him not to confront them alone."

Lila's voice is sharp. "And now you're protecting them?"

"I'm protecting myself," Jimmy snaps back. "You don't understand how long they've been running this town."

The door opens.

Sheriff Tom Granger steps inside.

Jimmy freezes.

The room goes still.

Tom takes in the scene, the photo on the bed, Jimmy's expression, then sighs. "That answers that."

Jimmy turns his face away. "I don't want to talk."

Tom nods slowly. "That's your right. But it won't stop what's coming."

Lila steps closer to the bed. Her voice drops, deadly calm. "It's time you do what's right, before you can't."

Jimmy squeezes his eyes shut. "They'll kill me."

"Apparently, they already tried," Lila fires back.

Tom clears his throat. "That's enough."

He turns to Amelia. "I need to collect the evidence the hospital staff pulled from his clothing."

"I'll walk with you," Amelia says. "Lila, will you pick up Edna and Bailey and meet me at the diner?"

Lila nods and waves her to go on.

Jimmy's voice cracks behind them. "I'm sorry."

Amelia pauses at the door. "I know."

Tom and Amelia leave the room and head to the nurses station in silence.

"Excuse me, I am Sheriff Granger, here to pick up the evidence that the doctor left for me," Tom informs the nurse on duty.

"Oh, yes, it's right here," as she reaches under the desk and pulls out a bag. "There is also a report or paperwork the doctor left for you," as she hands him a manilla envelope.

Tom takes both, he nods his head, "Thank you so much."

"No problem. You have a nice day, Sheriff!"

As they walk away, Tom stops, "I need to get to the station, but I would like you to meet me there."

"Sure I will head straight there," Amelia assures him.

Back at the station, Tom spreads the evidence across his desk, Jimmy's bloody jeans, the bullet the doctor's removed, Jimmy's phone, and other clothing he was wearing.

He exhales sharply. "I can't believe I forgot it."

"What?" Amelia asks.

"I never ran the serial number on the shotgun in the cabin," Tom admits. "Hank logged in the gun from Eric's death as Eric's without any verification in the report." His jaw tightens. "I'm correcting that mistake now."

Amelia holds up her hand, "Great, but I need to meet the ladies and Bailey at the diner, fill me in after?"

He nods as he picks up the phone. "And until we have arrests, Jimmy gets a deputy outside his door. Twenty-four seven."

Amelia nods. "Good."

Tom meets her gaze. "This stops being a theory today."

Amelia, sighs and nods, then heads toward the door.

Meanwhile, Lila is back at the Inn to collect Edna and Bailey. The sky has shifted into that familiar Kansas gray, heavy with expectation.

Bailey leaps into the car, panting and bright eyes.

Edna looks nervous but determined. “Did he talk?”

“A bit, but not enough,” Lila grunts as she shakes her head and rolls her eyes.

They head toward the diner together.

The diner is buzzing with lunchtime chatter when they arrive.

Edna picks a spot and Lila slides into the booth beside her, scanning the room. “This town’s secrets need their own wing at the hospital.”

A nearby nurse overhears and snorts before she can stop herself.

Dottie brings over menus and leans in. “You girls look like trouble.”

“We’re full of something,” Lila replies sweetly. “But we’ll take pie.”

Amelia appears from behind Dottie, “Absolutely, pie is just what I need, with a side of coffee, please.”

“You got it, coffee and pie all around, be back in a few minutes,” as Dottie heads back to the counter.

Amelia takes the open end of the booth after she finishes greeting Bailey and has a few licks on the cheek.

As Bailey settles under the table, Amelia catches movement near the window, a reflection that vanishes too quickly to be certain of what or who it was.

Her pulse quickens.

Whatever's coming next, she knows one thing for certain:

They're done hiding.

22

Threads of the Past

Amelia, still a bit on edge, sips her coffee and finishes her pie. Bailey is stretched beneath the booth, chin resting on his paws napping. Edna peers over Lila's shoulder, who is halfway through a story involving a disastrous school-author visit when Amelia's phone vibrates against the tabletop.

It is Tom calling.

"Hey," she says, keeping her voice steady.

"We've got something," Tom replies. His tone is different, focused, charged. "Ruiz stayed late last night going through the old banking records."

"What kind of something?" Amelia asks.

Lila stops mid-sentence. Edna looks up.

"The kind that doesn't stay buried anymore," Tom says, "When you are all done, come to the station."

"Will do, be there in minutes," she replies and hangs up.

Amelia stands, while putting some cash on the table, she announces, "I'm heading to the station, for news!" She pauses. "Actually, Edna, you should come with me. Lila, please take Bailey back to the Inn and we will come straight there afterward with the all the details."

Lila nods, "Yes, absolutely. Let's get moving!"

They all get up, throw on their coats, and head for door. Bailey scampers out first and is waiting by the door when Amelia opens it.

The wind is whirling as they exit the diner, heading to the Sheriff's station. The bitter cold air instantly turns their cheeks and noses red. Lila and Bailey hop into her car, just outside the door.

Amelia and Edna increase their pace, partly due to the cold and the rest due to their need to know what has been uncovered. Finally, they get to the station.

Amelia pulls the door open, against the wind and keeps a hold of it so Edna can get inside.

They immediately see Ruiz standing beside a whiteboard cluttered with names, arrows, and account numbers. He looks tired but satisfied.

"Welcome, ladies! You are all going to like this, we finally cracked the coded deposits," Ruiz explains. "Shell accounts. Cash-heavy. Hank Ross and Marcus Groves were both tied to them. Not just before Eric died but *after*. For years."

Tom folds his arms. "They didn't stop when Eric did."

Ruiz taps the board. "Two weeks before Eric's death, thirty thousand dollars disappears from one account. No record of transfer. No withdrawal. Just gone."

Amelia's breath catches. "That matches the cash found in the cabin bag… and the safe-deposit box."

Ruiz nods. "Eric likely skimmed it. Or tried to."

Edna presses a hand to her mouth. "He was trying to get out."

"And that," Tom says quietly, "is what got him killed."

Silence settles like dust.

"We can prove financial crimes," Ruiz continues. "The codes in these notes are about the smuggling and distribution of drugs. We also verified the prints on the money and drugs, both have Marcus' and Eric's prints on them. And, now possibly attempted murder in Jimmy Dale's shooting."

Tom stands. "That's enough to arrest Hank and bring him in."

"And Marcus?" Amelia asks.

"A warrant's already been issued," Tom replies. "I am charging them both with attempted murder until we sort out which one did it. We don't know if he's running yet, but we're about to find out."

"In the meantime, ladies, please head back to the Inn, I promise to keep you updated as this moves forward," Tom assures them.

Amelia looks at Edna and they agree.

Amelia pulls into the Inn's driveway, she and Edna have hardly said a word on the way. Both taking in what they have heard and anticipating what comes next.

Something's wrong.

The deputy's cruiser isn't parked where it should be. Lila's car is not here.

She's out of the car before the engine fully stops. The front door is ajar.

Her heart stutters. "No... no, no."

"Bailey?" Her voice cracks as she yells for him.

She rushes inside.

"Bailey!"

A blur of brown and black comes flying down the hallway, nails skidding on the wood floor as Bailey barrels into her legs, tail wagging furiously.

"Oh, thank God." She drops to her knees, burying her hands and face in his fur. "You scared me half to death."

Behind her, the deputy steps in from the back door, looking sheepish. "Sorry, ma'am. Your dog alerted me. Wouldn't stop barking."

Amelia looks up sharply. "Alerted you to what?"

"I thought someone might be out back. I checked the property. Nothing there. Or no one."

Her unease doesn't fade.

"Next time," she says carefully, "lock the front door."

"Yes, ma'am."

Bailey gives a low huff and plants himself at her side, watchful.

Edna has just caught up, as she hears the last of the exchange. "I am so glad everything is all right," as she sighs and takes off her coat.

"Also, Ms. Lila dropped off Bailey and said she would be back shortly for dinner," the deputy informs them as he heads back out the kitchen door.

Amelia starts opening the cabinets and pulling out supplies, glad everyone is safe, but the tension is not letting go.

"Here, let me help, we can whip up some dinner in no time," Edna offers.

Amelia smiles, "That would be great, smell of food cooking should be just the trick."

"Agreed, it certainly relaxes me. Oh, I think we still have some cobbler left over too, I will pop that in the oven and reheat it for our dessert," Edna proclaims.

Suddenly, the front door swings open and the welcome sound of Lila making an entrance brings a smile to Amelia's face and another sigh of relief.

"I'm back, hope I didn't miss anything," Lila announces as she enters the kitchen.

"Nope, nothing really, we are just getting some dinner and dessert going," Amelia replies.

Amelia's pocket starts ringing, she pulls it out and holds it to her ear to answer it, "Hi Tom, is everything okay?"

"Yes, I forgot to tell you something at the station, are the other ladies with you?"

"Yes, Lila and Edna are here, I will put you on speaker—okay, go ahead."

"Hello, ladies. So the license information for the shotgun from the wall at the cabin came back."

Lila raises a brow. "Well, what about it?"

"That shotgun is registered to Eric, not Jimmy," Tom announces.

"It WAS *Eric's*," Amelia says under her breath.

Edna closes her eyes. "Then it couldn't have been an accident, he would have been hunting with his gun if he was really hunting."

"Exactly!" Amelia agrees. "His gun has been hanging on the cabin wall this whole time. Jimmy's story doesn't hold."

"Yes, so that sheds a new light on things, we are going to start looking for another shotgun, the one that should have been put in evidence a decade ago," Tom states.

Lila exhales slowly. "Hank has been covering this all up, for years."

"But not anymore," Amelia says.

"I am going to let you ladies get to dinner. I will check in later," Tom says and hangs up.

Lila reaches across the table and squeezes Edna's hand. "Tom's different. He'll get to the truth this time."

Amelia hopes she's right. "Also, Lila, we need to fill you in on what Ruiz and Tom showed us at the station. Let's get this dinner on the table and then we can talk it all through.

Bailey lifts his head and stares at bowl as Amelia fills it.

The ladies sit around the table and discuss all they have learned today. Bailey finishes his food and moves over to lay on his blanket and keep watch on the door.

The threads are tightening.

23
Trouble at the Inn

The sun rises on the Inn. After some rather gloomy days, the sun has made it through. The blinding rays pierce the thin curtains and light up the entire kitchen. After a peaceful overnight, it is time for the favorite part of Amelia's day: breakfast.

"Good morning," Amelia greets her guests as they enter the kitchen. The omelets are hot and ready on the griddle, and the smell of the fresh bacon stacked high on a serving platter in the middle of the table calls everyone toward it.

"Well, a Good Morning to you too," Mrs. Kent replies. "I see you are in much better spirits today."

"Yes, had a very good night's sleep, and I feel refreshed," Amelia admits.

Mr. Kent chimes in, "It is good to see you as we have all been talking about how much has been on your shoulders and how well you've coped. Glad you are recharged."

Amelia nods and smiles as she passes the bowl of fresh cranberry cinnamon muffins to the table.

Bailey gives a perky bark as Lila flies into the kitchen, "Sorry, meant to get in here sooner." She grabs the coffee pot and makes rounds filling or topping off all the cups.

"Understandable, we all needed the sleep," Edna chimes in. "I think that is the first restful sleep I have had in weeks."

"Lila and Edna, before I forget, Dottie called me early this morning and asked us to all come by the diner after we are done with breakfast, does that work for you?"

Both Edna and Lila agree, with nods and smiles, as they work to finish their own breakfasts.

The three of them clear up the dishes and clean everything in record time.

Amelia pulls out her phone and sends a text to Tom: *Just letting you know that Lila, Edna, and I are going to run by the diner per Dottie's request. Then we will be back at the Inn.*

"Let's go, ladies. I'll drive," Amelia announces as she flings her coat on. Bailey starts to join them, but Amelia gives him that look, the one where he has to stay behind. He finds a spot in the parlor and curls up for a nap.

A little later, outside the Inn. Ruiz has been keeping a watchful eye, while Bailey has been patrolling inside.

Ruiz doesn't like quiet.

Not the peaceful kind, not the kind that settles naturally over a place. This is, the wrong kind, the kind that presses too close to the ears.

He makes his third slow loop around the Maple Leaf Inn, boots crunching softly over the gravel path that leads around the back of the house. The late afternoon air smells sharp, cold enough to sting his lungs. Bailey had been restless earlier, pacing near the windows shortly after the ladies left for the diner.

Ruiz had experience trusting dogs' instincts.

Then, it happens, a crash shatters the silence.

Glass explodes somewhere near the front of the house. Bailey's bark is loud and persistent.

Ruiz pivots and runs.

As he rounds the corner, he catches sight of a man in a dark hoodie scrambling over the low porch railing, landing hard before bolting toward the tree line behind the property.

"Sheriff, I've got a runner," Ruiz barks into his radio, already giving chase. "Male, average build, heading east toward the woods."

The man is fast.

Branches whip at Ruiz's arms as he barrels after him, boots slipping in damp leaves. The suspect glances back once, just long enough for Ruiz to catch the flash of fear in his eyes, then veers sharply and disappears into the thick trees.

Ruiz skids to a stop, breath burning in his chest.

"Lost him," he growls into the radio. "Requesting backup."

Minutes later, sirens are shrilling through the air as Amelia's car pulls into the Inn's driveway.

Her heart drops.

Deputies swarm the property in all directions. The front window of the Inn is shattered, only jagged edges are visible around the window's edge.

"Oh no," Edna gasps. Lila rolls down the window to get a better look.

Amelia slams the brakes. "Bailey!"

"He's fine," Ruiz calls out, jogging toward them. "A deputy is with him inside."

Her head falls back as she sighs with relief. "What happened?" Lila demands.

"Brick through the front window," Ruiz explains with a scowl across his face. "While I was checking the back. Whoever it was took off into the woods."

He gestures toward the porch. "There was something else, you should all come inside."

As they all make it through the front door, Ruiz directs their attention to the table inside the parlor where a brick sits, wrapped in brown paper. "I was just on my way in here to check this out."

Ruiz lifts it carefully, revealing the message scrawled in thick black marker:

THIS IS YOUR LAST WARNING.

Edna presses a trembling hand to her mouth.

Amelia's skin tingles all over, "They're escalating."

Ruiz nods. "One of the deputies radioed in. He found truck treads near the road about half a mile out. Look fresh. I'm heading there to take casts."

He radios Tom as he turns away. "Heading to get casts, before it gets too dark. I'll let you know if they seem to match the previous ones."

"Got it, I am heading there now," Tom replied.

Amelia grabs Lila and Edna's arms. "Come on, we are going in the kitchen so we don't disturb anything and I can hear Bailey whimpering." She guides them to the kitchen where a deputy is holding onto Bailey.

"Ma'am, I am keeping him in here so he doesn't step on any glass," the deputy explains.

"Thank you so much," as Amelia takes his collar and walks him over to get his leash. "Here, boy, let's keep this on you and we will sit in here with you."

Bailey leans against her leg, as she rubs his head.

"I am putting on some hot water for tea, anyone need anything else?" Lila asks.

"That sounds great, thank you," Edna answers as she removes her coat and sits down at the table.

Amelia is quiet, her thoughts taking over as she listens to fire on the stove and the water in the kettle starts to move. She is thinking about all that is happening. Who is the one doing all this? Is it Sheriff Ross? Is it Marcus? Or is someone helping them? Too many questions and not enough clarity.

Then, the kettle screams, it causes them all to jump. "Wow, we were all happy and content at breakfast and now we are on the edges of our seats," Lila breaks the silence as she heads to the stove.

Amelia adds, "You are right, we are back in it, definitely time for some tea," she gets out he mugs and also brings the rest of the muffins to the table.

"Thank you, I didn't grab one of those at breakfast, but it sounds perfect with tea," Edna says as she settles in and grabs a muffin.

Lila pours them all tea and takes a seat herself while also letting out a sigh, "Here we go, time to try and settle down again."

Amelia, still in thought but aware enough to acknowledge them both with a grin as she takes a sip of tea. Bailey curls up at her feet.

The front door opens, they all look toward the hall. It's Tom, his face looks like stone, he walks straight into the parlor. They lose sight of him as he leaves the hall, but they can all picture him in their mind—checking out the scene.

He surveys the damage, takes a look at the note, pulls out his radio and starts issuing orders for emergency boards to be brought in, then assigns two deputies to stay overnight. When he finally enters the kitchen and sees Amelia, his expression softens, a bit.

"We've got Hank," he says quietly. "Picked him up an hour ago. He's at the station."

Amelia's pulse spikes. "Has he talked yet?"

"Haven't questioned him yet, but we have him for the financial crimes, drug trafficking, and suspicion of murder for Eric Hampton's death," Tom replies. "This time, he's not walking out."

Lila folds her arms. "About time."

Amelia adds, "Well, I doubt this stunt was Hank then; so I wager the harassment has been Marcus?"

Ruiz walks in, dirt smudged across his uniform. He holds up a plaster cast.

"Tracks match the cabin site," he says. "Same tire width. Same wear pattern."

Lila lifts her teacup with prim satisfaction. "If the tracks fit..."

Tom doesn't smile, his eyes harden. "Someone's running out of places to hide, and you're right: it's likely Marcus."

"I'm heading home. You're in good hands for the night, it will be a long day tomorrow." Tom tips his hat to them and heads out the door.

The sound of crumbling gravel pierces through the moment of silence. The crew of two young men, strapped with a tool box and boards, walk toward the Inn.

Lila looks at them as if they'd arrived to hang holiday decorations. "Well," she remarks, "that was exciting."

"Let's not make it a habit," Amelia cautions, sweeping glass into a dustpan. "Hand me the broom?"

They work in concert—Lila sweeping the pieces that made it to the foyer, Amelia tidying, and Bailey supervising with intense canine interest. The Inn, obliging as ever, begins to right itself around them. The draft through the broken window stirs the cinnamon candles to a livelier flame.

It is not long before the flame settles, as the repairmen place the last board. "All done ma'am."

"Thank you both for coming so quickly and handling this mess," Amelia says as she waves good bye and they return to their truck.

"You're welcome. Hope the evening is peaceful," one calls out to her as they get in and then pull away.

Night settles in after the repairs are finished. The guests have returned, been briefed by Lila, and are now retired for the evening. Lila and Edna also said their good-nights and went upstairs for sleep.

The Inn, altered now, violated.

Amelia retreats to her office with Bailey and a hot cup of tea; she closes the door, and pulls the copy of Eric's accidental death file from her desk drawer. Her hands a little unsteady as she spreads the pages across the blotter.

She stares at the photograph.

The shotgun lying beside Eric's body.

Her breath catches.

The butt of the gun, there's a deep gouge along the wood. A scrape that shouldn't be there.

Her mind races.

She grabs her phone and pulls up the hunting photos with Jimmy, Eric, Hank and Marcus. She Zooms in on each of the guns.

There it is.

Jimmy's gun.

The same scrape. Same scar.

Her heart pounds as understanding slams into place.

The book. *The Picture of Dorian Gray.*

Not just a hiding place.

A message.

Someone who looks one way... while their true self remains hidden.

A chill crawls up Amelia's spine.

"Oh..." she whispers.

The guilty man isn't who he appears to be.

All this time, they've been looking at the wrong person.

That's what Eric was trying to tell his mother.

Bailey rustles beneath her.

Amelia doesn't notice.

She finally understands it all.

24

The "Confession"

The morning came and went without Amelia recalling most of it. Her mind is fixed on her revelation and getting the truth to come out. She has not told anyone yet. Lila and Edna are still in the kitchen sipping their coffee and the guests are out on their daily adventures.

Amelia is wiping down the kitchen counter when her phone rings.

It's Jimmy Dale.

She stares at the screen for a long moment before answering.

"Amelia," Jimmy says quickly. Too quickly. "I need to talk to you. Alone."

Her grip tightens around the phone. "You're in the hospital, Jimmy."

"I know. That's why it has to be now. Before… before something else happens."

She closes her eyes briefly.

"I'll come," she says. "But this is the last time." She hangs up and faces Lila.

Lila doesn't argue when Amelia explains.

She nods once, eyes sharp. "You want Bailey to stay here?"

"Yes," Amelia says. "With you and Edna."

Bailey whines softly as Amelia grabs her coat.

She kneels, presses her forehead to his. "Guard duty, boy."

He butts her hand with his nose, then settles, watching her leave with too-intelligent eyes.

⁂

Jimmy's room is dim, the pale thick curtains half-drawn. The deputy stationed outside nods grimly as Amelia enters.

Jimmy looks pale, shaken. Afraid.

Or very good at appearing so.

"You shouldn't have come alone," he says.

Amelia pulls a chair close to the bed and sits. "You asked for privacy."

"I'm scared," Jimmy says. "After what happened at the Inn... the threats. I don't think Hank's the only one who knows things."

Amelia studies him quietly. "You said you wanted to talk."

He swallows. "I do. I can't keep this in anymore."

She pulls her phone from her pocket. "Then I'm recording."

Jimmy hesitates, a fraction too long, then nods. "Fine."

She presses record.

"Start from what you told us before," she says calmly. "About the gun in the cabin."

"It is mine," Jimmy says quickly. "Always was. I couldn't hunt after Eric died. Just didn't have the stomach for it, so I left it there."

Amelia gives a small nod. "Go on."

He exhales, launching into it.

"Eric was working for Hank and Marcus. Smuggling. Cash runs. Off-the-books deals. Eric wanted out. Took money to fund his escape. Thirty thousand dollars."

"He asked me to meet him at the cabin," Jimmy continues, voice cracking. "Said he needed to talk. To figure out how to leave town."

Amelia keeps nodding, doesn't interrupt.

"While we were meeting at the cabin, Hank and Marcus showed up," he explains. "Eric told me to run. I didn't want to, but he insisted. I got outside, and then—"

His voice breaks.

"I heard the shot."

Amelia's expression doesn't change.

"Hank staged it," Jimmy continues. "Made it look like an accident. Shut everything down. Nobody questioned him."

Jimmy wipes his eyes. "The day I disappeared; I went back to the cabin. I had proof. A metal box. I hid it there years ago."

Amelia's pulse ticks faster, but her face stays neutral. "I assume you are talking about the box we found in the fireplace when we are out looking for you?"

"Yes, Hank found me," Jimmy says. "I dropped the box when I ran. He must've burned it."

Silence fills the room.

Then, Amelia asks, "What about you getting shot? It wasn't a shotgun, the bullet they pulled out came from some type of handgun. Where were you and who shot you?"

"I really don't remember, I was somewhere in the woods, I was trying to get to you to tell you the truth I'd been holding on to. It could have been either one of them. I am sure they both want me silent. It was dark too. I wish I could say how it was," Jimmy explains as his brow sweats even more than it was in the beginning.

"If you were in the woods when you were shot, how did you make it all the way to my back door without them catching up with you?" Amelia questions further.

Jimmy stares at her, then responds, "I don't know, I guess I was scared enough."

Amelia reaches forward and turns off the recording.

"Thank you," she says softly. "For trusting me."

Relief floods Jimmy's face. "You believe me, don't you?"

She stands. "I said I'd listen."

"That's not an answer," Jimmy pleas.

"It is all I have to say at this point, I have to get back to the Inn," she turns and leaves his room.

Amelia exits the hospital and doesn't return to the Inn.

She drives straight to the Sheriff's Office.

Tom looks up when she enters, immediately reading her face. "I already heard you went to see Jimmy, the deputy phoned me."

She sets her phone on his desk. "Jimmy confessed, I recorded it."

Tom exhales. "That's big."

"It's also a lie," Amelia says without a hint of a smile, dead serious.

Tom blinks. "You're sure?"

"Yes."

She paces once, then stops. "He confessed *too neatly*. He put Hank and Marcus front and center, made himself the frightened bystander."

Tom frowns. "That doesn't make it false."

"It does when the details don't line up," Amelia replies. "The gun in the photo with Eric's body, the one with the scrape. The other gun in the cabin, which you now know belonged to Eric, but Jimmy just lied and said it was his. The book Eric hid his letter in. The way he's always just close enough to the truth without touching it."

She directly looks Tom in the eyes. "Jimmy didn't run away that day, in fact, it is highly likely Jimmy was a part of killing Eric or even the one who actually shot Eric."

Tom's jaw tightens.

"There is no way he was not involved, although my gut turns at the idea." She continues, "He claims he only heard the shot, I think that is the lie and that he knows exactly what happened to Eric."

Tom leans back slowly. "Then, we let him keep talking."

"Yes," Amelia agrees. "We let him think he fooled us."

"Also, besides listening to that 'confession', you also need to look at the shotguns in those pictures I sent you from the bar—the ones with Marcus, Hank, Jimmy and Eric in hunting gear, holding their guns. Compare them to the photo of Eric's 'accidental shooting' scene, then you will see who that missing shot gun belongs to."

Tom's phone rings, he holds up a finger to Amelia.

"Sheriff Granger."

A pause.

He gazes at Amelia, his brows move inward, then one rises.

"You're sure?"

Amelia looks up from the chair across the desk and leans toward him.

Tom slowly sets the phone down.

"That was the lab in Topeka," he says.

"What did they find?"

"They finished examining the evidence from the hospital, the bullet removed from Jimmy's leg and the clothing he had on."

Amelia leans in more.

Tom exhales.

"Entry angle is downward. Powder burns on the denim indicate extremely close range."

He hesitates.

"Within inches."

Amelia's stomach sinks.

Tom continues, "The analyst said it's consistent with a self-inflicted wound."

Silence fills the office.

Amelia's eyes widen, "So Jimmy shot himself?"

Tom shakes his head slowly.

"No," he cautions, "He *may* have."

Amelia slumps a bit and sighs. "That shot that bothered me, it was too far away to really be shooting at Jimmy, I think it was to make us think someone was after him."

Tom adds, "You could be right, but right now, it only means he was closer to the gun than he told us."

"Okay, got it, but that is something," Amelia insists. "I knew something was off, but maybe there are more lies in his 'confession.'"

Amelia stands up abruptly and heads out the door, she turns back and adds, "I almost forgot, sending you the recording," as she pulls out her phone and sends it to him.

Tom only gets in a nod before she disappears.

Outside, the station she stops, she scans Main Street with quiet purpose. A few people heading into the antique store, a few boys skate boarding in the bank parking lot, a mother convincing her daughter to hold her hand as they prepare to cross the street, Amelia takes it all in. The everyday things which ground her and remind her what she loves about Maplewood.

For the first time, Amelia feels it, the end drawing closer.

And the truth, finally, running out of places to hide.

25

The Interrogation

As Amelia is getting into her car, her phone starts vibrating in her pocket.

It's a text from Tom: *You left so fast, I didn't get a chance to tell you. I am interviewing Hank in about a half hour. You should come in and at least watch.*

She replies: *I will be back.*

She then calls Lila.

Lila answers her call. "Hey, how did it go?"

"The meet with Jimmy went well, but Tom is interviewing Hank in about a half hour. Is it okay if I grab a coffee at the diner, go to the interview and then head back to the Inn after?"

"Yes absolutely, we'll whip up a dessert to eat while you fill us in on everything, when you get back."

"Deal," Amelia grins and hangs up.

Amelia arrives at the diner door as the call ends, she hesitates for a moment, then pulls the door open. The chime sings, Dottie's head turns toward her, "Well, hello, come on in and find a spot. I'll be right over."

Amelia smiles and gives Dottie a wave, she takes off her coat and plops down in a booth, sinking into the cushion as she exhales.

"Well, you look like you need a coffee, am I right?" Dottie asks as she approaches the table.

"Yes, that sounds great. Just need a few minutes to relax."

"I will be right back with that."

"Oh, Dottie wait, do you have some paper and something to write with I can use?"

Dottie, turns back, "Sure, I'll bring it back with your coffee."

Amelia nods and smiles.

Amelia takes in the atmosphere, calm, full of little conversations surround her. Just what she needs. It took all the energy and restraint she had not to lay into Jimmy while she listened to him string his web of lies. A moment to not think about it all, to stop figuring and relax.

"Here you go, hon," Dottie sits the cup down in front of her and pours a piping hot cup of brew.

"That smells great, thank you," as Amelia reaches for the cup and then wraps her hands around it. The warmth of the cup further soothes her soul.

"Oh, here is that paper and a pen," as Dottie sets it on the table, she also bends down and leans toward Amelia. "I don't know if you heard, although you probably did, they have

Hank in custody and the whispers are it is a pretty big deal," she whispers.

"Oh yes, I heard. In fact, that is where I am going next. I need to make some notes on this paper, things to make sure we get answers to. Tom is expecting me to come by," Amelia confesses.

"Wow, all right then. You drink that coffee and relax. I can't wait to hear what happens." Dottie heads away, toward another table.

The time slips away, the coffee is gone, her notes are finished and it is time to go. Amelia gets out some cash and sets it on the table, composes herself as she puts her coat on.

"Bye, Dottie, thanks for the coffee," Amelia calls out as she waves and heads out the door.

The wind is crazy now, the chill cuts straight through. The leaves are fluttering and flying down the road as she walks back to the station.

As Amelia enters the station, voices rise behind the closed interview-room door.

She doesn't need to clearly hear the words to know the tone.

Tom steps out when she knocks, loosening his tie, jaw tight.

"Perfect timing," he murmurs.

"Well, well, well. Is the innkeeper still playing detective?"

Tom turns, expression going flat. "That's enough, Hank."

“Hank has been just telling me how I am wasting my time and his,” Tom tells Amelia as they both take a seat across from Hank.

Hank Ross leans back in the chair like he owns it, boots stretched out, arms crossed, mouth curled into a smug half-smile.

“I should’ve known that you are probably the reason I am here,” Hank says, eyes glaring toward Amelia. “You seem to be good at sticking your nose where it doesn’t belong.”

Amelia doesn’t respond.

Tom places his phone on the table. “This is not an interview, yet,” Tom announces. “Amelia is here to share something with us, that you should hear.”

Hank snorts and stands. “Then get me a warrant. I am not interested in what she has to say.”

Tom moves faster than Hank expects, blocking Hank from exiting the room.

He pulls the folded paper from his pocket, unfolds it, and lays it on the table. “Already have one,” he gestures for Hank to return to the chair.

Hank’s smile falters.

“Arrest warrant,” Tom continues evenly. “Financial crimes, obstruction of justice, conspiracy to commit murder.”

He cuffs Hank and pushes him back into the chair.

“Sorry, Hank,” Tom says quietly. “You’re not going anywhere.”

Hank lunges forward half an inch, then slumps back. "You don't know what you're doing."

Tom stands again and steps into the hall and motions to a deputy. "Confirm Jimmy Dale's room is under full guard. No exceptions. No one is to visit him."

When he returns, "Amelia, coffee?"

She doesn't argue, just shrugs.

Tom pours two cups in silence.

"So Hank, we have something for you to listen to, Amelia recorded this conversation this morning, which is why she is here," Tom instructs him and presses play.

Jimmy's voice fills the room, everyone is silent as it begins.

Hank scoffs after the first sentence.

Then his face changes.

"Jimmy," he snarls. "That little..."

Tom stops the audio and waits a moment. "You should hear it all before you comment." Then, he hits Play again.

Jimmy's story continues, then stops.

The silence stretches.

"I am going to leave you for a minute with your thoughts, when I return, we will begin your interview. I am sure you are going to want to tell us your side of this mess," Tom informs Hank, as he and Amelia leave the room.

Tom shows Amelia to the next room, "Have a seat in here, while I deal with Hank."

"Okay, but I wrote down a few things to definitely make sure you ask him about if he doesn't mention them on his own," she hands him the list.

"Thanks, don't worry, we will get all the answers we need. I'll be back after the interview," Tom closes the door and re-enters the interrogation room.

As Tom sits down, Hank slams his cuffed hands on the table. "You want the truth? Fine, first that is all a load of crap."

Tom puts his hand up to stop Hank, starts the recorder and reads him his rights, "You understand?"

"Yes, of course I do," Hank barks back.

Tom lays out all the financial papers they have put together, the report showing Eric owned the shotgun, the flimsy "accident report" Hank handled, a copy of the letter Eric wrote his mother, copies of the hunting photos showing Hank with Eric, Marcus, and Jimmy a decade ago.

"Here is what we have at this point, besides the recording you just heard, we have everything we need to show your participation in the financial gains, which we are assuming at this point came from drugs. We know the shotgun in the cabin was Eric's and that it was not his gun in the pictures you took of the 'accident'. So you are going to jail. All that's left now is to determine if murder will be added to that sentence," Tom informs him.

"Okay, now tell me what isn't correct with Jimmy's statement and what really happened to Eric."

"Jimmy owns that bar in Brenton and is behind all the drugs," Hank snaps. "Always has been. Marcus is his muscle. Eric was his delivery guy. We are all disposable to him."

"Eric was running drugs," Hank continues bitterly. "But he thought it was for Marcus. Jimmy likes staying out of sight, playing the friendly mechanic, keeping his hands clean."

Hank laughs harshly. "Eric figured it out. Tried to quit. Took money to run."

"And you?" Tom asks quietly. "What was your role in all this?"

"I covered it up," Hank admits. "Moved reports. Killed scrutiny. Laundered cash. Because Jimmy had proof I'd skimmed city funds for years and back then, keeping that hidden seemed the most important thing to me."

He leans back, eyes burning. "I retired to get out. Thought I could disappear."

"And Eric's death?" Tom presses.

Hank shakes his head. "I didn't kill him. I swear that. I cleaned it up after, but either Jimmy or Marcus pulled the trigger. Since I was phoned to handle it, I can't say who actually killed him because I wasn't there until it was over. Jimmy told me to 'make it look like an accident.'"

The room goes still.

Hank's voice drops. "I'm not dying for him. I have done some things that are wrong... criminal, but I have never murdered anyone.",

Tom nods once.

“What about the shotgun, the one in the picture lying next to Eric?” Tom asks.

“Pretty sure, it belongs to Jimmy. I told him it was a mistake not letting me put it in evidence. He insisted he wanted it back. Apparently, his father gave it to him, so he wouldn’t part with it. I am sure that is the one that he used to kill Eric, it had blood spatter on it when I got there and took the photos. I gave it to Jimmy later. I have no idea what he did with it after that,” Hank explains.

“What about Jimmy’s accusation that you found him at the cabin and burned a metal box of evidence?”

Hank shakes his head in response, “That is pure fiction. I was nowhere near the cabin when Jimmy was running around trying to tie up his loose ends. My guess is that he searched every inch of that cabin to find it. It wasn’t proof he hid. He was trying to find the evidence that Eric had. I heard you already found the money and drugs that Eric hid. Jimmy looked everywhere for them a decade ago. Obviously, he finally found the records Eric had hidden and he burned them himself.”

“Do you have any knowledge of Marcus’ role in all this? You mentioned he was Jimmy’s muscle,” Tom inquires further.

“It would be speculation on Marcus’ current role, but I do know he threatened me on Jimmy’s behalf on many occasions, the blackmail threats and reminders to keep quiet came from him.”

“All right, is that all you want to say?” Tom asks Hank.

"Yes, I want to call my attorney now."

Tom stops the recording. "Sounds like a good idea, I will have a deputy help you with that." He takes the recording and evidence with him as he leaves the room.

Tom opens the door where Amelia is waiting and signals for her to come with him. Tom guides Amelia to his office, "I just want to talk with you for a moment, before you go."

They enter his office and sit down, "Sure, I am not in a hurry."

"Look, this is all coming together, mostly because you wouldn't let it go," Tom starts. "That's not a bad thing and I'm not upset at all. You were right about the pictures. I looked through them after you left. Jimmy is definitely the one holding the gun that was left by Eric's body and now Hank just confirmed it belonged to Jimmy."

Amelia, starts to speak, Tom raises his hand for her to wait.

"Look, I am glad you and the others are okay, but I don't want this to drag on any longer. I don't want all of you in any more danger. Please go back to the Inn and stay put, we are going to find Marcus and get him into custody," Tom explains.

"I am glad it is coming together and yes, we will all be safe," she assures him.

Tom walks Amelia to the door and braces it as she goes through, "The wind has really been picking up."

The night air is even colder now. She takes a deep breath, despite how cold it is, and as she exhales, she realizes the truth is finally visible now. A small grin appears on her face, Jimmy Dale's world is about to collapse, finally.

26

Spilled Coffee and Chaos

Tom doesn't relax as they stand outside station.

Amelia notices, his shoulders tight, his gaze constantly moving, hand hovering near his radio.

"Actually, since you aren't in a hurry, let's grab food," he says. "Then you go straight back to the Inn. No detours."

"Food is a great idea, I am hungry, but that sounds a bit ominous," Amelia replies.

"It is," Tom says plainly. "Marcus is still on the loose."

Before Amelia has a chance to reply, they spot Lila and Bailey outside the hardware store, Lila carrying a small paper bag and Bailey trotting proudly at her side like a four-legged escort.

"Well, if it isn't the town's entire investigative unit," Lila says brightly. "What'd I miss?"

Tom slows. "Everything's starting to come together now."

Bailey's ears perk up.

"That's comforting," Lila says.

"Did you get my text?" Lila asks Amelia.

"Oh, no, my phone was on silent."

"It's okay, you know now. I was just telling you I realized I needed to go to the store, so Bailey and I were going to do that while we were waiting on you," she explains.

"Well, I guess we are all going to dinner at Dottie's then," Tom chimes in.

They head into the diner together, the bell jingling cheerfully as it does, this time, wildly out of sync with the tension Tom is projecting.

Dottie slides coffee onto the table without being asked. "You all look like you've seen a ghost."

Tom doesn't sit or respond to Dottie. His attention elsewhere. He bends down to Amelia's ear, "Listen to me carefully. Once you're done here, you all go straight back to the Inn. You stay inside. Lock the doors. We're done whispering now."

Amelia nods. "I understand."

The words I *will obey* do not leave her mouth.

Bailey is standing next to Tom, instead of finding a cozy spot under the table, his ears raised and staring through the window.

Outside, an engine roars.

A pickup truck blasts past the diner windows, tires screeching as it barrels down Main Street.

Bailey explodes into motion.

He leaps toward the door, barking furiously, nails skidding across the tile.

"Bailey—!" Amelia shouts. Bailey stops at the door but continues barking.

Lila jerks back in surprise, her fresh cup of coffee sloshes across the table, spilling over the edge and soaking the floor.

Tom is already pulling the door open, "Stay, boy!" glancing at Bailey.

"Everyone stay put," he orders, sprinting out the door.

Amelia watches him tear toward his cruiser, radio crackling as he shouts into it for backup.

Her pulse races and her hands are clammy, she wipes them on her jeans.

"Amelia," Lila says sharply. "Don't."

Bailey whines, urgent, insistent.

She whips out her keys and runs out of the diner with Bailey in tow, going back to the station for her car.

Tom is already in pursuit, heading toward the edge of town.

Lila and the others in the diner are pressed against the windows and the talk is frantic.

Amelia's car is the next thing to pass by the diner, in the direction Tom was heading.

Moments later, just outside of town, Amelia sees the vehicles.

The pickup lies on its side at the edge of the road, one wheel still spinning uselessly. Tom's cruiser is stopped in the field, just beyond the truck, with the door standing wide open.

Amelia pulls over and jumps out of the car, Bailey leaps out with her.

Empty.

"No," Amelia's hands covering her mouth and her head darting back and forth, searching.

Bailey takes off, before she can stop him. His nose is low—he has the scent.

"Bailey, wait—!"

He doesn't.

She follows him, without any thought.

He freezes a moment, ears tilted back, his tail down, then he bolts toward the trees.

She moves carefully now, ducking behind tree after tree, heart pounding as distant voices echo through the woods.

Shouting.

Angry. Desperate.

Bailey's bark cuts through it, sharp, focused.

She spots shadowy figures ahead. Bailey is nearing them.

Then she hears them clearly.

It's Tom.

And another man.

Bailey speeds up and then launches himself at the figure, as the man turns.

The man stumbles backward, arms flailing.

Tom doesn't hesitate.

He tackles him, slams him into the dirt, cuffs snapping shut.

"Marcus Groves," Tom snarls. "You are under arrest."

Marcus spits dirt and a few profanities.

Tom radios in. "Suspect in custody."

Relief crashes through Amelia, her knees feel weak but she steadies herself.

Tom turns the moment he notices her presence.

His face is pale. Furious. Shaking.

"What the hell were you thinking?" he roars.

Amelia stands her ground. "You were alone."

"You were told to stay back!"

"You'd do the same for me," she fires back.

The words hang between them.

Tom drags a hand through his hair. "That doesn't make it right."

"No," Amelia agrees quietly. "But it makes it human."

Bailey trots back to her side, his tail wagging, chest puffed with pride. Amelia squats to greet him with a hug and a smile.

Tom exhales hard. "That dog's getting a medal."

Amelia almost laughs, but her legs are still trembling.

Marcus is in custody.

But the night isn't done with them yet.

27

Justice and Closure

Before Amelia heads to the station, she calls Lila, "We are all fine. Marcus has been arrested and we are heading to the station."

Lila lets go of the breath she was holding when her phone rang, "Thank God! Hang on a sec. Hey, everyone! They are all okay and they got the bad guy!"

Amelia hears the applause through the phone. "Will you meet us at the station?"

"Absolutely, see you there!" She leaves money on the table and has her coat and scarf on in a flash.

Marcus Groves sits alone in the holding room, hands cuffed, jaw clenched so tight Amelia can see the muscle bulging in his cheek.

The adrenaline has drained now, leaving behind something heavier.

Final.

Tom steps into the hallway beside her. "You should go home. All of you."

Amelia shakes her head. "Not yet."

Tom studies her for a moment. "This is my job now."

"I know," she says evenly. "But Marcus has what Hank didn't. And he knows it."

Tom frowns.

"Hank talked," Amelia continues. "But he protected himself. Jimmy's 'confession' does the same thing. Use both of their stories."

Tom's brows knit together, then lift slightly.

"You want me to play them against each other."

She nods. "I just know Marcus knows something that will help prove Jimmy is the one who killed Eric, if he sees that the others are lining him up to take the fall—I think he will be motivated to share what he knows. I doubt his loyalty extends to taking a murder wrap."

Tom stares at her. Part disbelief, part admiration. "You should've been a prosecutor."

She shakes her head and grins a bit, "No thanks! I prefer owning an Inn."

Tom places his hand on her shoulder. "I get it. So I'll do that. Really, I have this."

"Come on, let's go to the Inn," Lila begs Amelia as she grabs her arm and pulls at her toward the door. "That dessert is waiting for us and you have a story to share,"

Amelia gives in. "You're right. Let's go, Bailey. Tom, please let me know how it goes?"

"You know I will," as he nods and waves.

Amelia, Lila, and Bailey leave the station to head back to the Inn.

Tom heads into the holding room, Marcus looks up when Tom enters. Tom lays a file and recorder on the table and opens it to the picture of Eric's body. He starts the recorder and reads Marcus his rights.

"Do you understand these rights as I have explained them to you?"

Marcus nods.

"I am going to need you to answer verbally for the recording."

"Yes," replies Marcus.

"Would you like an attorney present for this interview?"

"No, I am not planning on telling you anything, so you might as well not bother."

"All right, let's start with you listening and then you can decide if you have anything to say."

Marcus remains silent.

"Hank Ross has given a statement," Tom says. "So has Jimmy Dale."

Marcus snorts. "Figures."

"Jimmy implies you and Hank were there and that one of you shot Eric, while Hank insists he was not there and did not kill him," Tom continues calmly. "Unfortunately, Hank cannot say whether you or Jimmy or both of you were there or which one of you killed him."

Marcus freezes.

"But," Tom adds, "Hank does say you work for Jimmy, that you have threatened him over the years on Jimmy's behalf. So, it doesn't seem a far stretch that you would kill Eric to protect Jimmy?"

Marcus leans back, eyes narrowing. "And if I say nothing, since it sounds like you just have a lot people talking, but no way to prove who shot him?"

Tom's gaze hardens. "Well, since you all seem to agree it wasn't an accident as previously reported, then you can all take the murder charge together, but my guess is someone is going to provide the evidence to prove they didn't do it, the question is, is that going to be you?"

Silence stretches. Marcus stares downward at the floor then upward to the photo in front of him.

"Just so you know, jail time for threats, vandalism, and your role in the sale of drugs is less severe than murder or even conspiracy to commit murder, so maybe it is time to think about where you end up in this mess," Tom offers.

Marcus still silent but then his head rises and he looks straight at Tom.

Marcus exhales. "Jimmy pulled the trigger."

Tom doesn't interrupt.

"He always stayed clean," Marcus mutters. "Friendly mechanic. Everybody liked him. He let Hank take the heat and forced him to cover it up. Had dirt on him skimming city money."

"And Eric?" Tom asks.

Marcus' voice drops. "Eric wanted out. Took money. Thought he could disappear. Jimmy found out and wouldn't let him leave."

"Were you there when he killed Eric?"

"No," Marcus says. "Jimmy told me after. He told me about the 'accident story' and that Hank gave him his shotgun back after he finished the report, just so there would be no real evidence tying him to it."

Tom's expression tightens. "So where is it now?"

Marcus gives a short, bitter laugh. "Still hidden, unless Jimmy got nervous and moved it."

Tom says nothing.

Marcus leans forward, lowering his voice. "You want proof? Go to Jimmy's shop. The service pit in the main bay, the one under the old hydraulic lift. There's a compartment built into the sidewall below the grate."

Tom's eyes narrow. "A compartment?"

Marcus nods once. "Jimmy had it made years ago. Said it was for cash and parts he didn't want anybody finding. Mostly, he used it for the shotgun."

"And you know this how?"

"Because I helped build it," Marcus snaps. "Jimmy wanted it hidden deep enough that nobody poking around would notice. You have to pull up the loose metal panel on the left side once you're down in the pit."

Tom stays very still.

Marcus continues, his voice flat now. "He kept more than the gun in there. Drugs too. Sometimes cash. Whatever he didn't want out in the open."

Tom watches him carefully. "Why tell me now?"

Marcus gives him a dead-eyed stare. "Because Jimmy thinks everybody else is supposed to go down for him. Hank talks, I take the blame, and Jimmy keeps smiling like he's the victim. I'm done with that."

"Well, isn't Jimmy also a victim? He was just shot and is still in the hospital."

Marcus laughs.

Tom's eyebrows almost meet in the middle. "Is that funny?"

"That's just what he wants you to think. I didn't shoot him. I was the one in the woods who fired the rifle, to make everyone think he was being shot at."

Tom pauses, "All right, we can look into that. In the meantime, if that gun is still there," Tom says evenly, "this gets much worse for him."

Marcus shrugs against the cuffs. "Good. It's about time."

"One more question, did you shoot Jimmy the other night, payback maybe?"

"No, that was Jimmy's last attempt to lead you all in another direction. He thought if he was a target you would start looking for someone else."

"So if it wasn't you, who shot him?"

"He shot himself, with his handgun. I was nearby though. He had me wait in the woods and then once I heard sirens, I was to fire a shot into the air with my gun."

"I see, well the report confirmed that Jimmy's wound appeared self-inflicted, so I guess that tracks, but he didn't have a gun on him when he was rushed to the hospital. Do you have that or know where it is?"

"Nope. I guess he stashed it somewhere, probably near the stream behind the Inn. That is where he said he was going to do it and then make it up to the Inn."

"Anything else you want to add to this?"

Marcus shakes his head, "No. Honestly I'm glad it's over."

Tom closes the file. "Thank you."

Back at the Inn, the lights are low.

Lila, Edna, and Amelia are sitting at the table in the kitchen. Bailey curled up at their feet. The house is quieter than it has been in days, no tension buzzing under the surface, no sense of being watched. Amelia has just finished filling them in on Bailey's outstanding bravery.

"Come here, boy," Lila calls to Bailey.

He jumps up, tail wagging and puts his paw on her knee.

"This is for you, our four-legged hero," as she gives him bite of their blueberry pie. Bailey laps it up immediately and curls back up on the floor.

"You are spoiling him," Amelia says and then grins.

"He deserves it, he has been our rock during this whole nightmare," Edna adds.

They continue to finish their desserts and enjoy their teas, but Amelia keeps checking the time every few minutes. She knows Tom is handling it, she is on the edge of her seat, waiting for news.

About an hour later, a quick knock on the door and then, "It's me," Tom announces as he enters.

He walks straight to the kitchen, doesn't sit.

"It was Jimmy," he says simply.

Edna gasps and her hands immediately land on the sides of her face.

"All three are being charged," Tom continues. "Hank and Marcus for their roles, laundering, obstruction, conspiracy. But both gave testimony placing Jimmy alone with Eric at the time of his death. Neither was anywhere near the woods when it happened."

Edna presses a hand to her chest.

"And Marcus gave us something else," Tom adds, looking at Amelia. "Something I'm following up on tonight. If it is where he says it is, then we'll have the physical proof to put this to bed for good."

Amelia straightens. "The shotgun?"

Tom gives one grim nod.

"Ruiz is bringing Jimmy in from the hospital now," he continues. "By morning, this will be over."

Tears slide silently down Edna's face.

"Justice is being served," Tom says gently. "Your son made mistakes, but he realized it. And he tried to walk away."

Edna nods through her tears. "That's the son I'll remember."

Tom turns to Amelia. "This wouldn't have been solved if you hadn't been willing to look and then seen what others missed."

Amelia swallows. "I just listened to the woman who knew Eric best, his mother."

"That's rarer than you think."

Tom starts to head out, but then stops and turns back. "Actually, do you mind if I take Bailey outside for a short walk?"

Bailey knows the word walk, and in seconds he is at Tom's feet, tail wagging and panting. Amelia, with a confused look on her face, "Sure. Do you want his leash?"

"No, not necessary. Come on, boy!" Tom heads out the kitchen door with Bailey in tow.

The two of them walk down the back yard hill until they are about a yard or two from the edge of the stream. Then Tom stops and kneels next to Bailey. “Hey, buddy, I need your help,” pulling a bag from his coat pocket and opens it. “Take a whiff. Find it, boy!”

Bailey starts smelling the ground, he noticeably has a scent and starts to head closer to the stream, turns, going through some tall weeds to his right, out of sight. Then, three sharp barks.

“Good boy, I’m coming!” Tom joins Bailey in the weeds, kneels down and starts searching with his flashlight and hands across the ground. “That’s it!” Tom pulls something out of the weeds, puts it into his other jacket pocket. “Good boy,” he rubs Bailey’s head, just the way Bailey enjoys it. “Let’s go.”

As Tom opens the kitchen door and steps in, Bailey is on his heels, “He has quite the nose. He found Jimmy’s handgun in the weeds by the stream.”

“There he goes again, our little detective on the case,” Lila exclaims as she hugs Bailey and fluffs up his fur. Bailey proudly accepting the accolades.

“Good boy,” Amelia grabs a treat and gives it to him, which he takes and trots off to his bed to savor it.

“Thank you. That is what I needed to confirm Jimmy shot himself. I will get this to the lab tomorrow for official confirmation.

“How did Bailey find it?” Edna asks.

"I had him sniff Jimmy's shirt in the evidence bag. He tracked the scent right to it," Tom explained. "I better get home. I have an early start tomorrow."

All the goodnights are said and Amelia walks Tom to the front and sees him off.

Sleep comes easily tonight.

For everyone; well, almost everyone.

28

The Hidden Compartment

The town is asleep when Tom pulls into the lot behind Jimmy Dale's shop.

His headlights sweep across the familiar building, catching the dented garage doors and faded sign out front before he kills the engine. Ruiz parks beside him a second later, another deputy behind him. The night air cuts cold and sharp, and for a moment nobody moves.

Then Tom reaches for the warrant on the seat beside him and gets out.

Ruiz joins him at the rear entrance. "You think Marcus told the truth?"

Tom looks at the darkened garage. "He told enough truth tonight that I'm not betting against him."

Ruiz gives a short nod.

Tom unlocks the back door with the key taken from Jimmy's personal effects at the hospital. The lock clicks. The door groans inward.

The smell hits them first.

Motor oil. Metal. Rubber. Old grease worked into concrete over years of labor.

Tom switches on the overhead lights.

The shop awakens in sections, long fluorescent bulbs buzzing one by one until the garage is washed in a pale industrial glare. Tool chests line one wall. Tires are stacked in neat towers. A battered calendar hangs crookedly near the office door.

Everything looks ordinary, except for the temporary repairs to close up the broken window from the break-in.

That is what Tom hates most.

He walks toward the main service bay, then points, "There, Marcus said, under the old hydraulic lift."

A deputy brings over a flashlight while Ruiz crouches near the grate. "This one?"

Tom steps beside him and looks down. The service pit sits beneath the lift like a dark slit in the concrete floor, covered by heavy metal plates.

"Open it."

Together they drag the first plate aside. It scrapes across the floor with a harsh metallic scream.

Then another.

Cold, stale air rises up from the pit below.

Ruiz shines the flashlight down. "Ladder's intact."

Tom takes the light. "I'm going down."

He climbs carefully, boots striking the metal rungs one at a time until he reaches the narrow floor below. The walls are poured concrete, stained with years of use. He sweeps the beam across the left side.

At first, he sees nothing.

Then—

A seam.

Barely visible.

A rectangular outline in the wall, cleaner than the concrete around it.

"Ruiz," he calls upward. "He was right."

Tom crouches and runs his gloved fingers along the edge. One section gives way slightly under pressure.

A loose panel.

He wedges his fingers beneath it and pulls.

The metal shifts with a soft *pop*.

Behind it is a dark cavity, deeper than he expected.

Tom angles the light inside and goes still.

There it is.

A shotgun wrapped in an old canvas cloth.

Beside it, several vacuum-sealed packets. White powder and pills. Brick after brick tucked into the space with efficient care. A metal cash box. A stack of bundled bills.

For one long second, nobody says anything.

Then Ruiz's voice comes down from above. "Sheriff?"

Tom keeps staring into the compartment. "Call it in."

Ruiz doesn't ask why.

Tom carefully lifts the shotgun first and unwraps it enough to see the stock.

Walnut. Scratched along one edge. Distinctive dark mark near the butt.

He had seen it already.

In the hunting photo Amelia made him study.

And again in the crime scene photo lying near Eric Hampton's body.

"We've got it," Tom says quietly.

Ruiz exhales above him. "And the drugs?"

Tom shines the beam over the stash again. "Enough to bury him."

He hands the shotgun up first, then the packets, the cash box, and the bills. Ruiz bags each piece carefully while the second deputy photographs everything in place. Tom remains in the pit until the last item is removed, checking the compartment twice more to make sure nothing is missed.

When he finally climbs out, his knees ache and his jaw is tight.

Ruiz zips the evidence bag closed around the shotgun. "Marcus just handed us the whole case."

Tom shakes his head. "No. Jimmy did. He kept it."

He looks once more around the garage, at the clean counters and neat tools, the ordinary face Jimmy Dale showed the town for years.

Then he says, "Bring him in."

⁂

By the time Jimmy arrives at the station, the sky has gone from black to charcoal gray.

He no longer looks like the frightened man in the hospital bed.

He looks tired.

Pale, yes. Weak from the gunshot wound, yes. But the panic is gone now, replaced by watchfulness. Calculation.

Ruiz guides him into the interview room while Tom stands waiting with the file open on the table.

Jimmy lowers himself carefully into the chair, wincing as he settles. His gaze flicks from Tom to the recorder to the evidence bags on the far corner of the table.

And stops.

He recognizes the shape of the shotgun before Tom says a word.

His whole body stills.

Tom sits across from him. "You asked Amelia to record your confession."

Jimmy swallows. "I told the truth."

Tom says nothing for a moment.

Then he reaches over and drags the evidence bag closer, turning it for the gun to show clearly through the plastic.

Jimmy's face drains.

Tom lets the silence do the work.

"That's not all." Tom signals to the door and Ruiz enters handing him another evidence bag, which Tom sets on the table too,

Jimmy's eyes widen—it's his handgun. He remains silent.

Finally, Tom says, "Let's see about that statement that you told the truth. We searched your shop and we searched the weeds near the stream."

Jimmy says nothing, but slumps into his chair, deflated.

"We found a hidden compartment in the service pit under your hydraulic lift."

Still nothing.

"In it, we found this shotgun. Your shotgun." Tom taps the bag once. "The same one in the hunting photo. The same one left beside Eric Hampton's body."

Jimmy's breathing grows shallow.

Tom opens the file. "We also found a large quantity of drugs, cash, and storage materials consistent with trafficking."

Jimmy closes his eyes briefly.

"Hank Ross gave a statement. So did Marcus Groves," Tom continues. "Both place you at the center of the operation. Both say Eric found out the truth and tried to leave."

Jimmy opens his eyes again and looks at Tom with something close to hatred.

"Hank's a liar."

Tom nods once. "He is. So are you."

Jimmy's jaw tightens.

Tom leans forward. “Your confession was neat. Too neat. You made yourself the scared bystander. You put Marcus and Hank exactly where they needed to be to absorb the blast. But then we found the gun.”

Jimmy looks away.

“You want to explain why the murder weapon was hidden in your shop?”

No answer.

Tom keeps going, voice even. “You want to explain why Marcus knew exactly where it was? Why Hank identified it? Why you lied about the cabin, about Eric, about everything except the parts that helped you?”

Jimmy’s shoulders sag, slightly.

Not surrender.

Just damage.

“You think I killed him for thirty thousand dollars?” he asks at last, voice low and rough.

Tom doesn’t blink. “I think you killed him because he stopped being useful.”

Jimmy laughs once, without real humor in it. “That’s what they said?”

Tom folds his hands. “That’s what the evidence says.”

The room goes quiet.

“You know what else the evidence says? You shot yourself in an attempt to continue the deception, but the lab confirmed it was self-inflicted. We located the gun you used to do it—which I am sure the lab will confirm that too.”

Outside the door, a phone rings somewhere in the station. A deputy's footsteps pass and fade. Dawn presses faintly at the frosted window.

Jimmy stares at the table for so long Tom thinks he might say nothing else.

Then, at last, Jimmy speaks.

"He was leaving."

Tom says nothing.

Jimmy's voice is flat now, scraped clean. "Eric thought he could just walk away. Take the money and disappear. Start over somewhere else and leave the rest of us to deal with the mess."

Tom watches him carefully. "So you met him in the woods."

Jimmy gives one small nod.

"He said he was done. Said he didn't care what happened after. Said if I came after him, he'd tell everything he knew."

Tom's voice stays steady. "And then?"

Jimmy's eyes remain fixed on the table. "And then it happened."

Tom's expression hardens. "That's not good enough."

For the first time, Jimmy looks up.

Something flickers in his face then. Weariness. Bitterness. A long-held anger finally slipping.

"He was like a son to my mother," Jimmy says quietly. "Everybody loved him. Everybody forgave him. He got to dream about leaving. I got to stay here and clean up every mess."

Tom does not soften. "So you killed him."

Jimmy's mouth tightens.

Seconds drag.

Then he says, barely above a whisper, "Yes."

The word lands hard.

Tom does not move.

Jimmy continues staring straight ahead. "He turned his back on me. He thought I wouldn't do it. I grabbed the gun. He turned, I fired." He swallows. "It was fast."

Tom reaches over and switches off the recorder.

Jimmy doesn't look relieved.

He just looks old.

Ruiz opens the door a moment later, takes one glance at Tom's face, and understands enough not to speak.

Tom stands. "Jimmy Dale, you are being charged with the murder of Eric Hampton, along with additional charges related to narcotics trafficking, money laundering, conspiracy, obstruction, and honestly anything else that comes up as we close this case."

Jimmy gives a dull nod, as if the words are coming from very far away.

Then, before Ruiz leads him out, Jimmy says, "I want to see Amelia."

Tom studies him.

Jimmy lifts his eyes. "Please."

Tom's expression stays guarded. "Why?"

Jimmy swallows. "Because I want to ask her something."

Tom says nothing for a long moment.
Then, “I’ll tell her you asked. That’s all I’m promising.”
Jimmy nods once.
Ruiz leads him away.

29

A Community Healing

This morning's dawn is pale and quiet. The wind has even calmed to a gentle breeze.

Amelia and Edna stand by the stream, a bouquet of fall colored flowers divvied up between them. The water moves gently, sunlight dancing across its surface, the perfect backdrop for reflection.

Edna and Amelia release the flowers one by one.

"For peace," Edna whispers.

"For truth," Amelia adds softly.

"For Eric... for faith... for friends..." They continue as they drop the flowers into the stream.

They stand together, Amelia's arm around Edna, until the last flower disappears downstream.

They exchange a look, one of closure and even mutual admiration, then turn and head back to the Inn.

Back at the Inn, Lila leans in the doorway, coffee in hand.

"Well," she says brightly. "If we're officially a new agency, then I'm the new Snack Captain."

Bailey *yips* in agreement, tail wagging furiously.

Amelia laughs, shaking her head with her eyes closed.

And for the first time in a long while, Maplewood is quiet again.

Breakfast at the Maple Leaf Inn is different this morning.

Not quieter, livelier.

Amelia barely has time to refill coffee cups before another guest stops her with a smile, a congratulatory squeeze of the arm, or a whispered "*We're so glad it's over.*" The kitchen hums with the scent of warm biscuits and bacon, but there's something else in the air too.

Relief.

Lila, stationed at the end of the long table like a master of ceremonies, has clearly taken it upon herself to fill in any missing details.

"And that," she announces between sips of coffee, "is why you should never underestimate an innkeeper, a good dog, or a woman with pattern-recognition skills."

A ripple of laughter moves through the room.

Amelia shoots her a look. "*Lila.*"

"What?" Lila says innocently. "I'm being educational."

Bailey weaves between chairs, tail wagging, soaking up attention like a celebrity on tour.

Amelia is still in the kitchen when Tom arrives at the Inn later that morning.

The breakfast rush is over. The counters are mostly cleared. Lila is drying dishes and talking too much while Edna sits at the table with a cup of tea, looking more rested than she has in days. Bailey lies near the stove, one eye open.

All three look up the moment Tom steps inside.

"Well?" Amelia asks.

Tom removes his hat. "We found it."

She goes very still. "The shotgun?"

"And a hidden stash of drugs in the same compartment at Jimmy's shop."

Lila lowers the dish towel. "Well."

Edna closes her eyes.

Tom looks at Amelia. "Jimmy confessed."

No one speaks.

The only sound is the faint tick of the wall clock and the kettle settling on the stove.

Amelia exhales slowly. "Then it's done."

Tom nods. "It's done."

Edna presses her fingers to her mouth, eyes filling, but this time, something different in the grief.

Not shock.

Release.

Tom hesitates, then looking at Amelia says, "He asked to see you."

Lila spins around to face Amelia. "Absolutely not."

Bailey gets to his feet.

Amelia looks at Tom. "Why?"

"He said he wants to ask you something." Tom pauses. "I told him I'd ask. You do not have to go."

Lila sets the towel down with force. "You definitely should not go."

Edna says nothing. She just watches Amelia with quiet, searching eyes.

Amelia rests one hand on the back of a chair. "I think I should."

Lila throws up both hands. "Of course you do."

Tom steps closer. "If you go, you won't be alone. A deputy will be right outside the room."

Amelia nods. "Then I'll go."

The holding room is smaller than Amelia remembers.

Or maybe it only feels that way because Jimmy looks diminished inside it.

He sits at the table in a county-issued blanket draped around his shoulders, his face drawn, his hair disordered, his hands cuffed in front of him. He looks up when she enters, and for the first time since she has known him, there is no performance in his expression.

No easy smile.

No practiced concern.

Just a man with nowhere left to hide.

Amelia remains standing for a moment before taking the chair across from him.

"You asked to see me."

Jimmy nods. "Thank you for coming."

She doesn't answer.

He looks down at his cuffed hands. "Tom said you figured it out before anybody else."

"I suspected."

His mouth twists faintly. "No. You knew."

Amelia studies him. "Close enough."

Jimmy gives a tired little breath that might have once been a laugh. "How?"

She is silent for a beat.

Then she says, "Ultimately, I listened to Eric."

He looks up at her, brows crunching up, moving his head back and then rests his head in his hand.

Jimmy says nothing.

"Initially, the gun in the cabin didn't fit. Eric was staying there, but then he supposedly kills himself accidentally a distance from the cabin, but there is a shotgun still on the wall after a decade? It couldn't belong to someone else and still remain there."

His expression shifts a bit.

Not surprise.

Recognition.

"Eric put the note to his mother inside a book, *The Picture of Dorian Gray*, are you familiar with that book?"

"No, what does a book have to do with anything?"

"The book is about a man who appears charming and respectable to everyone around him," Amelia explains.

"But the truth of who he really is... is hidden."

Jimmy doesn't move.

Amelia holds his gaze.

"Eric wasn't hiding the book for comfort reading. He was leaving a message."

"The man everyone trusted... was the one destroying him, the one with the evil soul."

Jimmy's jaw tightens.

Amelia leans forward slightly.

"You were the only one living two lives, Jimmy."

Jimmy looks down again. "I almost had you."

"You kept it buried for ten years," Amelia says, "but you didn't silence Eric."

Jimmy closes his eyes for a moment.

"He left the clues that finally exposed you for who and what you really are."

That earns the smallest nod.

For a moment, the silence stretches between them.

"What I don't know is how Eric figured you out?" Amelia asks.

Jimmy shuts his eyes.

A muscle in his jaw twinges.

"I don't know, honestly, one day he came to me after he decided he couldn't do this and asked for my help getting away from Marcus and out of the drug scene. That is when he thought we were both in the same position, he even asked me to come with him. I assume later when he found the banking papers, he sorted out it wasn't Marcus and it was me behind everything."

Amelia shakes her head, "I guess that piece of the past will stay a mystery, but I assume there was a connection between Eric and Jonah, perhaps Jonah gave him the records. Based on Jonah's wife's recollection, he was troubled before his heart attack, he also held on to all those records, he likely wanted them to be found at some point."

"I guess, I underestimated how tight I kept things," Jimmy admits. "But why did you have to get into this and why did you ignore all the threats I had Marcus send your way?"

Amelia thinks of Edna by the stream. Of Lila in the kitchen. Of Bailey barking into the dark. Of Eric never getting the chance to grow older.

She stands.

Jimmy looks up at her, "Well?"

"Because the truth matters, just as justice does."

Jimmy lowers his head.

Amelia turns and walks to the door.

Behind her, his voice comes one final time, stripped of everything except exhaustion.

"Eric was my friend, you know?"

Amelia stops, but does not turn around.

"I know you think that," she says, "too bad your greed mattered more."

She closes the cell door behind her and nods to the deputy, who follows her out.

When Amelia returns to the Inn, Lila and Edna are relaxing in the parlor and Bailey is asleep on the hearth.

Before she can even say hello, her phone rings.

Amelia answers, listens, then sighs with fond resignation. "Yes, Mayor Tuttle. 1:00 p.m. at the diner. Of course."

She hangs up and turns to Lila. "We've been summoned."

"Oooh," Lila grins. "Is it a parade or a speech?"

"Lunch," Amelia replies. "Which means both."

"We should get ready and head there, I will fill you in on my visit with Jimmy in the car," Amelia says.

"Yes definitely do that," Lila agrees.

By 1:00 p.m., Dottie's Diner is packed.

The usual clatter of plates is layered with excited chatter, speculation replaced by satisfaction. Justice has settled in, and Maplewood is doing what it does best: talking about it.

Amelia, Lila, Edna, and Bailey have taken the corner booth, after passing by all of the high fives and thanks they received from everyone they passed.

Mayor Charles Tuttle stands near the counter, clearing his throat with the gravity of a man who enjoys an audience.

"Friends," he begins. "This town has been through more than its share of unrest lately."

A murmur of agreement travels through the crowd.

"But thanks to the diligence of our Sheriff's Office," he gestures toward Tom, "and the... persistence of one Amelia Hartford..."

A wave of applause breaks out.

A warm flush sweeps across Amelia's cheeks.

Lila claps loudest.

Dottie leans over to whisper loudly, "And don't forget who sent Edna her way."

Edna smiles softly from her seat, eyes bright, taking it all in.

"It's been a long road," Mayor Tuttle continues, "but today we celebrate closure, accountability, and community."

Bailey chooses that moment to hop onto an empty chair and swipe a biscuit straight off a nearby plate.

The room erupts in laughter and applause.

Tom catches Amelia's eye across the diner and gives her a quiet nod, no speeches, no theatrics.

Just understanding.

Edna leans over and squeezes Amelia's hand. "I'm glad I came," she says softly. "Answers make all the difference."

"They really do," Amelia replies.

Bailey crunches happily on his stolen prize, entirely unrepentant.

And for the first time in weeks, the diner hums not with tension, but with peace.

30

Reflections by the Stream

The stream moves slowly this evening, its surface catching the last gold of the setting sun. Amelia walks beside it with Bailey trotting ahead, nose low, tail swaying back and forth.

For once, she isn't thinking about evidence or suspects.

She wonders if that will last.

"Do you think trouble finds us," she murmurs to Bailey, "or do we just notice it when it shows up?"

Bailey pauses, glances back at her, then resumes his patrol of the tall grass. Clearly undecided.

Lila appears moments later, two paper cups in hand. "You attract mysteries like flies to jam."

Amelia laughs softly. "I was hoping for a quieter reputation."

“Too late,” Lila says cheerfully, handing her a coffee. “You’re memorable.”

Back at the Inn, a repair truck hums as the last pane of glass is set into place. The repairman gives Amelia a thumbs-up. “Good as new.”

As dusk settles, Tom approaches from the drive, hands tucked awkwardly into his jacket pockets.

“For Bailey,” he says, holding out a small leather tag.

Amelia clips it onto Bailey’s collar and reads:

Detective’s Assistant

Bailey sits taller.

Something outside catches his attention, he heads to the back door. There are a couple of raccoons scurrying toward the stream. Lila laughs. Amelia smiles, “Nothing to worry about. They’re just looking for dinner.”

For tonight, the town is quiet.

And that’s enough.

31
Renewal Abounds

The Maple Leaf Inn hums like a living thing.

The phone rings again as Amelia slides a tray of muffins onto the counter. She wipes her hands on a towel and answers with a practiced smile in her voice.

"Yes, we do still have availability for the Maple 'n Cider Festival… well, one weekend left… yes, it fills quickly."

She hangs up and exhales, half-laughing.

The reservation book lies open on the counter, its pages filling fast. Both festival weekends are nearly booked solid, names written in neat lines that make her heart lift. For the first time in weeks, the rush is exciting instead of overwhelming.

Bailey enters the kitchen and plops down at her feet, tail thumping once like punctuation.

"I know," she tells him. "Busy is good."

In the parlor, a new photo rests on the mantel. Amelia straightens it gently, Edna and a young Eric, both smiling, caught mid-laugh. It rests perfectly, right there, among the family photos and small treasures that tell the Inn's story.

A knock sounds at the door.

Josie steps inside, cheeks pink from the chill. "I wanted to stop by and say thank you," she says. "The town feels lighter. Like we can finally breathe again."

Amelia smiles. "I think we all needed that."

Josie hesitates, then adds, "We'd love to have you on the Maple 'n Cider Festival planning committee."

Before Amelia can answer, Lila breezes in behind her. "Yes, count us in!"

Amelia laughs. "Something light is exactly what we need."

Bailey accepts a hug from Lila with dignified patience.

Later, Tom stops by, out of uniform, jacket slung over one arm.

"Just coffee," he says. "No emergencies."

They share a quiet smile over steaming mugs, the kind that doesn't need explanation.

As he leaves, Lila leans in conspiratorially. "Oh! You won't believe what's happening at the old train depot."

Amelia raises an eyebrow, already grinning. "Let me finish breakfast first."

Bailey thumps his tail, ears perked.

The Inn buzzes. The town heals. And somewhere nearby, a new mystery waits its turn.

I hope you enjoyed this story! Don't forget to leave a review, it is greatly appreciated.

Use QR code to Leave a Review

If you want to be notified as soon as the next book is out, follow my author page on Amazon or sign up for my email newsletter by emailing me at: contact@angiestreetauthor.com

About the author

Having grown up in Kansas, where she has lived in the city and rural communities, it only makes sense for her stories to be set there. Now a grandmother, she has a lifetime of connections and experiences to draw from when creating characters who could be your neighbor or friend. In 2025 she decided to pursue a writing career, it was something she had thought about over the years but never took that first step. She loved cozy mysteries and puzzles from a young age, which is why she chose this genre. She loved the hometown atmosphere and friendships in these stories, but desired to put her own spin on them. In her books you may find perhaps a little more suspense, higher threat levels, light police procedures, and from time to time some criminal conspiracies. Just slightly pushing the outer edge of a cozy mystery.

In addition to writing, her time is spent enjoying her grandchildren, caring for her flower beds in the Spring and Summer, volunteering for various non-profit organizations, and helping with her husband's business. Dogs are also in her world, she has always had at least two dogs. Writing a dog into her stories seemed natural, who doesn't love an adorable helpful pooch. However, in real life her dogs only find dead animals in the woods, not people!

www.ingramcontent.com/pod-product-compliance
Lightning Source LLC
LaVergne TN
LVHW090555110826
845146LV00001B/132

* 9 7 9 8 9 9 5 6 1 4 5 1 7 *